The candid and ins
BEYOND MOT

provide validation for women who have chosen
to forgo motherhood as well as guidance for
those who are making decisions about it.

WOULD MOTHERHOOD SUIT YOU?

If you are currently trying to decide whether or not
to have a baby, don't postpone asking yourself this
question. Really think about it, starting now. It's
important to know as much as possible about your
feelings, your conflicts, your fantasies, and your
needs. Talk to your mate, talk to your friends, but most
importantly, talk to yourself—and listen carefully,
with an open mind, to what you have to say.

- How do you really feel about children? If you feel uncomfortable, is your reaction based mostly on inexperience—or are there other reasons?

- Do you think that some problem in your life—such
  as an unhappy marriage, depression, or poor self-
  esteem—will be solved by having a child? Remember
  that the only thing having a baby can solve is the longing for a baby.

- Think about your own childhood. What was good that
  you would want to repeat, and what was bad that you
  want to repair? Are you ready to confront your past
  in order to be a good parent?

- Is someone trying to talk you into pregnancy even
  though your heart is really not in it? Do you find yourself repeatedly making excuses not to have a baby,
  such as "we can't afford it right now"? Maybe you are
  trying to tell yourself something.

As Jeanne Safer writes, "No carefully considered decision, responsive to your real feelings, born of honest
self-examination, will be the wrong one."

Beyond Motherhood

Choosing a Life
Without Children

Jeanne Safer, Ph.D.

POCKET BOOKS

New York   London   Toronto   Sydney   Tokyo   Singapore

Note: Names and certain identifying information about the women who were interviewed for this book have been changed.

Ezra Pound: *Personae.* Copyright 1926 by Ezra Pound. Reprinted by permission of New Directions Publishing Corp.

An *Original* Publication of POCKET BOOKS

 POCKET BOOKS, a division of Simon & Schuster Inc. 1230 Avenue of the Americas, New York, NY 10020

Copyright © 1996 by Jeanne Safer

Library of Congress Cataloging-in-Publication Data

Safer, Jeanne.
    Beyond motherhood : choosing a life without children / Jeanne Safer.
        p.   cm.
    ISBN: 0-671-79344-6
        1. Childlessness—United States—Psychological aspects.
    2. Childlessness—United States—Case studies.   3. Women—United States—Psychology.   I. Title.
    HQ755.8.S24   1996
    306.874'3—dc20   95-46120
                                                                    CIP

First Pocket Books trade paperback printing February 1996

10   9   8   7   6   5   4   3   2   1

POCKET and colophon are registered trademarks of Simon & Schuster Inc.

Cover design by Patrice Kaplan
Cover art by Heidi Younger

Printed in the U.S.A.

*To My Mother and
the Memory of My Father*

Acknowledgments

I am grateful to the women whose stories comprise this book for giving so generously of their time and of themselves. Our conversations were moving and important to me, and I will never forget them.

The following people were of great help to me: my agent Lisa Bankoff, who demonstrated her enthusiasm by representing this book during her own pregnancy and has been invaluable throughout, both personally and professionally; my dear friend and colleague Judith Kaufman, whose comments on the manuscript were, like her, direct, generous, and unerringly astute; my editor Julie Rubenstein, who took a deep personal interest in the project; and my husband, Richard Brookhiser, who lets me be myself.

I beseech you enter your life.
I beseech you learn to say "I,"
When I question you;
For you are no part, but a whole,
No portion, but a being.

—Ezra Pound, *Ortus*

Contents

Beyond Motherhood

Introduction

THIS BOOK IS ABOUT MAKING A CONSCIOUS DECISION NOT TO have a baby—how to do it, how it feels, what it means, and the impact it has on your life. It grew out of personal experience, because this was the choice I made myself.

I spent years examining my feelings about motherhood, struggling with my ambivalence and my anxiety, until I eventually came to terms with how I felt about a course of action that had profound effects on virtually every aspect of my identity as a woman and a person.

Since I am a psychoanalyst, I had the advantage of training in the art of self-examination, which was an extremely valuable tool in resolving a question as emotionally charged as motherhood. I wrote this book in order to share the insights I gained through my own experience and to present the stories of other women who have made the same decision I did, in their own unique ways. My purpose is to provide help, both expert and deeply personal, to other women who are themselves struggling with the issue of whether they want to have children and support for those who have already decided not to and want to empathize with kindred spirits. Any woman who has felt ambivalent about motherhood—including many a mother—will find much here that resonates with her own experience. This subject is still not discussed openly very frequently, and many women feel quite alone with their doubts, as well as ashamed of having them in the first place.

In this book you will hear my story and you will meet an array of women of all ages from all over the United States who came to the same conclusion. Some of them knew from childhood that motherhood was not for them, and others still have lingering doubts into middle age, but all offer insights about what it really feels like to live this still unconventional life, what factors in their histories, personalities, and circumstances shaped their decisions, and what the myriad consequences were. These women talk with remarkable candor about their mothers, their marriages, their childhood memories, their thoughts about aging without offspring, their legacies, and the meaning of their lives. They describe how they have forged their identities as women without being mothers, and they share anecdotes both amusing and outrageous about other people's reactions to them. Their vitality, their passion for life and work, belie any stereotype of childless women as emotionally barren or unfulfilled. They provide guidance and inspiration for anyone who has grappled with this issue, regardless of her final resolution.

One of the biggest questions women who are in the midst of this crucial decision-making process ask is whether they will have regrets in the future if they decide not to have a family. The women in this book offer a variety of clearheaded answers. Despite the mixed emotions some of them continued to have, every one I spoke to emphasized that making an active choice to be childless, rather than postponing or avoiding dealing with the dilemma, was a source of pride for her. Each believed that understanding and accepting herself, even though she was acting contrary to expectations both external and internal, strengthened her self-esteem and freed her to pursue her life in the way that was right for her.

The Epilogue at the end of this book is specifically addressed to women who are still in the process of making up their minds. It contains practical advice based on the experience of others who have already made the choice and recommendations on how to think about whether a childless life would suit you: how to determine your real feelings about children and parenthood; how to evaluate your reactions, including your misgivings and your anxiety; and how to deal with the consequences.

I entitled this book *Beyond Motherhood* because it demonstrates that a woman's life can have expanded dimensions in the contemporary world outside the boundaries of the role that, until recently, was the sole widely acceptable one. Motherhood is no longer a necessary nor a sufficient condition for maturity or fulfillment. It is a biological potential and a psychological vocation which a significant minority of women, upon reflection, recognize does not suit them.

Throughout this book, I have intentionally avoided using the phrase "childfree," which has recently gained currency as a way to destigmatize childlessness, because I strongly believe that to deny that there is a loss involved is the wrong way to go about doing it. In my opinion, any woman who does not have a child—and I include myself—is missing something, whether she knows it or not. I will never have the unique relationship with a child that a mother has, and she will never have the degree of personal freedom that I have—we're *both* giving up something, and we are both getting something too. Neither of us "has it all," although we can both feel amply compensated and satisfied with what we have and the choice we made. Acknowledging the losses that life entails is an essential part of self-acceptance.

I believe that the stories in this book have relevance beyond the immediate issue of whether or not to have children, because they demonstrate the value of seriously and compassionately confronting your own life, your own needs, and your real feelings regardless of anything but truth. This is the basis for any valid decision and a key to conscious, creative living.

Part I

My Story

NOBODY WILL EVER SEND ME A MOTHER'S DAY CARD—ONE OF those Crayola-decorated creations made by dedicated, not fully coordinated small hands. I will never search my newborn's face for signs of my khaki eyes or my husband's aquamarine ones, or sing a lullaby. No child of mine will ever smile at me, or graduate, or marry, or dedicate a book to me. I will leave no heir when I die.

Now that infertility is so much in the news, this has become an increasingly familiar litany. But there is a difference in my case: I chose this fate. I made a conscious decision not to have a child.

Realizing that motherhood was not for me was the hardest decision of my life and the loneliest—marriage and career were easy by comparison. It also took the longest; I actively struggled with myself for over five years before I reached this conclusion. They were years of intensive and often painful self-examination, in which I confronted the most difficult things about my personality and my history and faced losses I could only imagine. What would society think of me? What would I think of myself? What would the shape and meaning of my life be without a family? And what would I leave behind as my legacy? Now, at the age of forty-seven, I look back in relative tranquillity on the process I went through. With pride and relief, and no more tears, I can say that I know that the course I chose was the right one for me. But it certainly wasn't clear at the time.

I.

I had always been ambivalent about whether I wanted a child, though it was an abstract concept until the circumstances of my life stabilized enough to make motherhood a real possibility and therefore a matter for serious, practical consideration. In my twenties, getting my Ph.D. in psychology, establishing a private psychotherapy practice, and finding a sane and suitable man to love were foremost in my mind.

Since my family is small, I'd had little contact with children when I was growing up. In college I worked as a counselor at a hospital for emotionally disturbed children and became close to a little girl there, but I was much more comfortable with the adolescents; I spoke their language.

I did have a fleeting longing to have a baby once, when I was involved with a man who lived far away. I knew it was our shared fantasy, a way to have part of him when I could not really have him. The desire dissipated, without grief, when the relationship did.

Then, at age thirty, I met Rick, a sweet-voiced, subtle-minded twenty-two-year-old writer in a singing group that performed Renaissance music on New York City street corners. When we married three years later, I was frank about my doubts: I told him I'd never felt a longing for babies, I feared I had an aversion to the whole idea, and I could make no guarantees that the balance would shift. Could he be happy without a family? He told me tenderly that what he really wanted and needed was me, regardless of what the outcome would be—which was one of the reasons I knew I had finally chosen the right man.

By the time I reached age thirty-five, I had to confront motherhood head-on for both our sakes. And it was no coincidence that I finally began to face my feelings about it when I reached the age my own mother had been when I was born, for it was then that my path was diverging from hers most concretely. Despite the profound influence that our complicated, bittersweet relationship had on my decision, she never pressured me or made me feel guilty for not providing the grandchildren she would have adored.

Even without her intervention, though, that damnable, hackneyed "biological clock" was ticking thunderously away, and my commitments were getting more numerous by the minute. It would have been foolhardy (and uncharacteristic of me) to leave something so momentous to chance, so a child had to be planned. In that case, life would have to change radically and I had better start making arrangements. But, I found myself thinking that fall, how can I consider getting pregnant when I have to teach at eight A.M. next semester? My practice is just starting to take off—I'll lose all the momentum if I cut back to part-time. That summer I thought, it'll have to wait until after we get back from Bali and I'm no longer taking medication to prevent malaria. And what about the trip to Turkey we want to take next summer?—you can't bring an infant to the Third World. Since my office is in our two-bedroom apartment, we would have to find a bigger place or I'd have to rent a separate space to see patients, but we couldn't afford the former and I hated the idea of the latter. And pregnancy seemed like such an ordeal. I dreaded feeling exhausted, nauseous (I'd been prone to it all my life), and distended. How would I ever lose the weight?

Then I ran out of excuses. I realized that this was one decision that was not going to take care of itself, unlike many others—since I'd chosen my profession at the age of ten—that this internal monologue was my way of postponing the moment of truth. Although I wasn't aware of it, I must have been afraid, not only of going through the process, but of what my conclusion would be. I must have been worried that I really didn't want to do it and what my unwillingness might imply. Nonetheless, since knowing as much about my own motives as I can has always been my credo and the foundation of my work, I had to pursue this, wherever it led.

My anxiety and resistance to figuring out where I stood made me understand why so many women in my position deal with their ambivalence either by plunging into pregnancy or by continuing to avoid it with unexamined excuses. What could be harder than choosing between forever and never? You can't give a baby back or (at least not easily) have one after menopause. And if you do decide not to have one, biology precludes reconsidering; if you discover at fifty that something fundamental is missing from your life because of this choice, you can't fix it—it would even be difficult to adopt then. Few things are as final, as irrevocable, as this. You can get divorced, change professions, or leave town, but not having a family takes you down a road where you can see that there's no going back.

The ensuing process of active consideration lasted into my early forties. I kept a diary during this period to assess where I stood and to express my uncensored thoughts. Whether to become a mother was a steady, subliminal pre-occupation during my days and filled my dreams at night. One of the first entries describes my predicament:

> I find it hard to write this, because it makes thoughts I hate to think concrete: after less than twelve hours in the presence of a happy, placid, beloved baby, I feel utterly incapable of having and enjoying a child of my own. The parents didn't seem to notice that we couldn't have a conversation. They weren't even impatient with the constant intrusion, while I felt furious and confined by it. All the paraphernalia, the exclusive (and legitimate) focus on the baby's moment-to-moment state, exhausted me. Rick was uncomfortable too, but he had an easier time with it because his temperament is more tolerant and accommodating—with the family and with me.
>
> I realize nobody is immune from mixed feelings, but mine seem so extreme. I feel so closed, so selfish, such a misfit. Why does something that seems instinctive in others feel artificial and unavailable to me? Am I unable to really give of myself, to be devoted? I know a lot can change in the five years I have left to deal with this. Thank goodness for my loving, sympathetic husband, who does not judge me.

Around the same time, I recorded a dream that symbolized my state of mind. Since teaching dream interpretation and using it to understand my patients is my professional specialty, I pay particular attention to what dreams reveal about my own inner reality. My dreams during this period were especially vivid and compelling because my mind was working overtime trying to solve my problem. Analyzing the language, themes, and symbols of my dreams provided clues to what I was feeling and, at the deepest level, why I was feeling it, a precious resource in a time of crisis:

> Last night I had one of the saddest dreams of my life. Rick and I saw a treeful of birds as we were walking on a country road. To my delight, I noticed that they were scarlet tanagers, a species more unusual and beautiful than I would have expected to see in such a place. Then I noticed that all the leaves of the trees—it was a forest of birches—had turned yellow. I was deeply disturbed, as if the time had slipped away without my knowing it. "But I'm not ready yet," I said frantically to Rick. "There's supposed to be at least another month of summer before this happens." Then I realized, with a cold shiver, that the trees stood in an old abandoned graveyard.

This was my first dream about motherhood, symbolized by the "family tree," which I would prematurely destroy by not having children. The image of the tree reminded me of the gnarled gray birch that grew outside my father's office window. The abandoned graveyard among the birches I understood to mean that I would be the last of his line; there would be no child of mine to visit my grave. My complaint that winter, the infertile season, was encroaching more quickly than it "should have" reinforced my awareness that time for consideration was indeed running out. I had been postponing dealing with my feelings because I wasn't yet ready to accept aging and dying like a barren, untended tree.

But there was a promise of transformation in the image of the unexpected red birds, which replaced the green leaves the trees should still have retained. The beautiful tanagers were not "born" organically from a tree the way its leaves are—the way a child is born from its mother's body—but had alighted from elsewhere to adorn it. They represented a different kind of creativity from the biological, an alternative tie to the future.

This dream confirmed that I had entered the phase of actively grappling with the question of motherhood, unconsciously as well as consciously. However, while the dream haunted me, I only dimly perceived its meaning and the resolution it anticipated while I was working so hard to make up my mind. In an effort to inject some rationality into my quandary, I began "researching" the topic by reading books and articles, including *Ever Since Eve* (famous women's experiences of pregnancy and birth) and *Having Babies in the Eighties* (a contemporary how-to manual), which I found interesting but not close enough to my own experience to be really helpful. I talked to my friends, both mothers and nonmothers, and to my own therapist. And I made lists of pros and cons and contrapositives, taking care to emphasize the satisfactions to be gotten from either outcome:

Reasons to Have a Baby

A new kind of intimacy
Pleasure in child's development
A sense of connection with life and with other women
Regaining my own childhood
Passing on what I love and know

Reasons Not to Have a Baby

Living by my own schedule
Uninterrupted privacy and intimacy with Rick

Freedom from continuous obligation
Focus on my own life and activities
Spontaneity

The Wrong Reasons to Have a Baby

To fit in
To prove I'm okay
To please my mother or Rick
Not to be alone in old age
To have somebody to leave my possessions to

The Wrong Reasons Not to Have a Baby

Pain of pregnancy
Awkwardness and ignorance about childcare
Fears of competition
Fears of mutual disappointment
Fears of turning into my parents

I tried my best to be logical and practical, to eliminate every obstacle I could think of. Just to be sure I wasn't agonizing for nothing, Rick and I were checked medically. The verdict: Conception was problematic but still possible. We even picked names—David and Ariel. And since it was essential to me not to be controlled by fear (I didn't want to feel I hadn't had a baby because I was too scared to do it), I went for a series of biofeedback sessions to teach myself how to manage my pregnancy anxiety, should I decide to go through with it. My gynecologist also reassured me that he would help me deal with my fears, as he had seen me through assorted medical anxieties for the last twenty years.

I was leaving no stone unturned. Still, despite occasional fluctuations—when a friend's toddler snuggled into my lap or a confidante cheered me on—my feelings hardly budged. Prospective parenthood seemed more like a minefield than a challenge. The diary entries at the beginning of every volume, at each new year and birthday—my times for ritually taking stock—were strikingly consistent over the years.

The theme that haunted me was my visceral discomfort around young children, how it made me feel about myself and what it meant. My years of therapy made me realize that I was dealing with something far deeper than annoyance at inconvenience, that my reactions had roots in my own past, in what children (and mothers) symbolized to me. It was probably related to my perfectionism, discomfort with the childish parts of myself, my own desire for exclusive attention, distress about the demands of being a parent, and, most of all, my relationship with my own parents. Everybody goes through this, I told myself; why should it stop me? Perhaps a deeper understanding of why it bothers me so profoundly will make it more manageable, help me separate fantasy from reality, and allow me to become a mother.

Rick and I discussed the topic periodically; usually I brought it up. The conclusion was always the same: that since I would be the one to go through pregnancy and because my life would change more radically, he believed that I had to decide whether motherhood was for me, as independently as possible of what he might want. The most overt thing he ever did was to point out little girls who looked like my baby pictures—"dark hair, big cheeks, and a determined air"—and tell me how delightful it would be to have a daughter who resembled me. But he frankly admitted his own ambivalence and uncertainty about whether he wanted to be a father and whether he would be good at it. He felt that any desire of his, as important as it was, could not be legitimately separated from my willingness. To insist would have been immoral, from his point of view, and he could be happy either way.

He knew, and he told me, that leaving so much in my hands also had the function of absolving him of having to make a decision himself. His stance permitted him to avoid confronting his own mixed feelings, preventing a wrenching conflict between us. I was immensely relieved by his position, which did much to assuage my guilt and allowed me to struggle unburdened, because I didn't feel I was robbing the man I loved of something he passionately wanted or needed. Once more, I marveled that there was nothing authoritarian in his nature and reflected on how lucky I was. But how ironic, I thought in my self-lacerating moments, that precisely those qualities that kept him from pressing me—attunement to another's needs, adaptability, a strong sense of justice—and which as a result ultimately prevented him from being a father, would have made him a wonderful one.

As I struggled with myself, I experienced no overt external pressure to reproduce. Still, I was amazed at how susceptible I was to something that seemed to be "in the air." Suddenly the city was teeming with strollers, and the sidewalks seemed thick with pregnant women. Everybody was doing it—and everybody was writing about it. I was bombarded by magazine covers of celebrities in their forties wringing their hands over infertility or proudly displaying their twins, ecstatic new mothers who had just discovered "the true meaning of life." Anybody I knew who wasn't trying to get pregnant was trying to adopt before it was too late.

I saw close up how urgent the desire could be when one of my patients who was my age discussed staying in a miserable marriage because she so desperately wanted a baby (happily, she left in time to meet a more compatible second husband). Why was I so different? No one I knew seemed as anguished or as unclear. If other women felt as I did, they were keeping it a secret.

"Baby lust" was incomprehensible to me even as it surrounded me. I started to feel like a different species from women my age who longed for children enough that they were willing to undergo humiliating invasive procedures in order to conceive or spend fifty thousand dollars to adopt. One friend who had endured nine years of unsuccessful infertility treatments confided to me how she wept with envy when she saw women with baby carriages in the street; I dared not tell her the same sight made me feel bombarded and invaded.

I finally had everything you were supposed to have to take the plunge into parenthood—marriage, money, some measure of maturity. So why did I cringe instead of glow when my gynecologist showed me the spot on his baby-picture-filled desk "reserved" for my offspring? How could I decline to join them? Why my jaundiced view? *What kind of a woman was I anyway?*

I was shocked and ashamed when I heard myself asking this question. Women had been liberated at least twenty years ago. Though I belonged to no official organization, I considered myself a card-carrying feminist. I had kept my name, and I made more money than my husband. I was adamantly pro-choice. Surely I of all people did not measure a woman's worth or her femininity by her fecundity. And yet, there it was, the voice from within, born from my immersion in a society that still, though more subtly, makes these judgments and has these expectations. A woman may be fine without a man, but the technical term for a woman without a child is still "barren," which implies that she is empty and lifeless within. There is no equivalently pejorative term for a childless man, and nobody, himself included, questions his masculinity.

My pain didn't come from the wrenching realization that maternity was physically impossible—that is another kind of grief. Not wanting a child is different from wanting one and not being able to have one. The intent of an infertile woman is not suspect, and her limitation is only physical; her capacity to love is intact. She wants what everybody is supposed to want, only her body prevents her from achieving it. The sense of defectiveness I battled was in my heart.

Despite feminism and common sense, I found it difficult not to feel ashamed about not wanting to be a mother or to feel fully feminine just as I was—with my plants, my cooking, my love of dancing, my profound satisfaction in caring for my patients and the people I love. What real woman voluntarily turns her back on reproduction or does not naturally want to take care of a baby? How can she put her own life first?

Every woman who is childless by choice has to battle the implicit assumption that she is unnatural or cold. I noticed that in every article I read on the subject, the voluntarily childless women were at such pains to point out that they liked children, which may indeed have been true but which they wouldn't have had to emphasize if there weren't some lingering doubt about their normality in their own, or their projected readers', minds. Although I knew that many women have children for the worst possible reasons and that many mothers are hardly paragons of mental health, it was shocking to discover this stigma within myself. "Selfish" is one of the most damning things you can call a woman, and "immature" is one of the most damning things I can call anybody. All this I had internalized long ago; nobody had to say these things to me.

Every time I watched the parade of Snuglis down the avenues, I felt like an outsider to the main preoccupation of my generation. People my age seemed happily obsessed with the accoutrements and activities of parenthood, and my life seemed radically different from theirs. There were times when I felt painfully alienated from my dearest friends, who now as parents, despite all we still had in common, inhabited a world I did not want to share. They sang its praises and either didn't appear to be oppressed by its constraints, or denied or suppressed any misgivings. They got up early and went to bed early and, of necessity, had less time for me.

In my own as well as other people's eyes, the action I contemplated branded me as different, forced me into nonconformity that derived not from a wish to rebel but from a realization that my prerequisites for happiness were outside the norm. I would be permanently out of sync. Just as I had never appreciated what it felt like to be handicapped until I had to wear a cast myself, this experience made vivid what it must feel like to live, volitionally or otherwise, as a homosexual, as single in a married world, as a foreigner. Being different can be immeasurably enriching, but it marks you. There is a price for the unconventional life.

As bad as I felt about it, something in me continued to rebel anyway. I saw that the biggest obstacle to motherhood for me was the very real upheaval it would wreak in my life and the intrusion and interference— the loss of control—that it represented. On the most overt level, I dreaded the ordeal of moving, reorganizing my complex agenda, interviewing and then cohabiting with housekeepers, restricting my activities. No more midnight suppers or daily exercise sessions, I thought, or concert series without elaborate planning, for twenty years. My time would never again be fully my own. My

19

resistance to all the necessary changes and conditions always seemed more compelling than any gratification I could anticipate.

I was particularly aware that children would change my marriage drastically. Until they went to college, we would no longer be alone together for extended periods, which was one of the chief pleasures of my life. When would Rick next read a book to me or go out to lunch with me? How often could we spend an afternoon in bed? Parenthood, I believed, would certainly spell the end of our nightly candlelit, sandalwood-scented bubble baths complete with silly bath toys, where we played like children in a deliciously adult incarnation. We wouldn't have the privacy or the time. A family is not a couple, and whatever its joys, unbridled intimacy is not among them.

Intimacy with another adult did not feel confining to me because, regardless of the time Rick and I spend together, I am not responsible for his life. He doesn't *need* me to be there as a child would; an adult is simply not dependent in the same way. I can be otherwise engaged for extended periods without feeling as if I'm abandoning or neglecting him; he can make dinner for himself, and he's better at being alone than I am. His autonomy and his maturity free me from obligation, compulsion, and guilt.

Despite my concerns, I did not feel entirely emotionally unequipped for motherhood. In fact, I knew I had some of the most important qualities a good parent needs—empathy, devotion, love of fun, strength, and steadfastness. But in some essential ways I seemed temperamentally unsuited for the job. As heretical as it was to admit it, I realized that having a child of my own would force me to spend a great deal of time doing things I disliked; I'd never been crazy about children's birthday parties when I'd attended them years earlier, and a trip to the circus is my idea of purgatory. My tolerance for noise and other people's messes is limited, and I recoiled at the chaos and limitations a baby would bring. I'd seen my friends' child-proofed apartments, their living rooms taken over by Nintendo and Ninja Turtles—"G"-rated videos and Sesame Street their primary forms of entertainment. I didn't want to be resentful or fastidious or controlling, but I was afraid I couldn't help it; either the child would be restricted, or I would. People differ in their capacity to accommodate intrusion and change in their emotional and physical environments. I'm at the low end.

I thrive on being able to do what I want when I want, unimpeded. To a rare degree, I have been able to construct a life on my own terms, and I loved the space, the lack of rigid planning, the order without regimentation. I couldn't ignore what I would be giving up (and what would take its place), and I saw that it simply would not be possible to continue to live my way and be a responsible parent—or a happy one. I spent years making my life the way it is, and I wanted to keep it. Despite what the women's magazines say, I couldn't see a way to have it all.

In addition to the necessary immersion in her child's world and the changes in her own, a mother takes on responsibilities and impingements of all kinds. Even in these days of involved fathers, she is almost always the one who gives more, who feels too guilty to go to work when the child is sick at home, who makes the arrangements, content though she may be to do so. Children must become her priority; she ceases to be a free agent. I thought of how much time my mother spent ferrying me to lessons, making meals, molding her schedule to mine. Her attention, availability, and involvement were points of justifiable pride to her. I didn't doubt that I, too, would do what a child needed—I doubted I could do it with good enough grace. I anticipated a bruising conflict of interest between devoting full enough attention to my child or myself. I knew of creative, accomplished women who combined careers and families—it didn't stop Madame Curie—but I couldn't imagine where they found the energy.

More than my own psychology is involved here. Women really *do* have to put many of their needs aside for their children, especially in the early years. Society tends to deny the price that mothers pay and idealize the sacrifices they make, rationalizing it all as part of feminine instinct, which makes it extremely difficult for women to acknowledge any resentment they feel. Satisfied mothers may be less prone to resentment because they largely identify with their child's requirements and feel sufficiently compensated.

All of this might have seemed manageable, or might not have loomed so large, if I had felt the same sense of vocation for parenthood that I did for my profession. Becoming a psychotherapist also entailed years of labor and sacrifice, not a little tedium, and a major curtailment of freedom. Because it was my goal and my passion, I never begrudged the effort. But with a baby, I wasn't at all sure that mother love would conquer all.

My fortieth birthday was fast approaching, and I still hadn't definitively decided. "Am I meant never to see my own child unfolding before my eyes?" I wrote in my diary. "Is my life enough just as it is? Maybe I should just stop using birth control and let fate decide."

A series of metaphorical dreams about trains let me know what a trip on the "mommy track" really felt like to me. These dreams compared deciding to have a baby to catching a train. In both cases, once you're on you're on; you relinquish control of your own momentum for the duration of the journey, and you can't get off between stops. In the first dream, I decided to catch a train just as it was pulling out of the station even though I feared it wasn't the right one, and realized I'd be crushed if I did— a warning of the hazards of an impulsive decision.

Despite my apprehension, several of my friends urged me to reconsider and made compelling arguments to support their case. One in particular, who had herself decided not to have a baby years earlier, did not want me to miss out as she felt she had and was convinced that I would enjoy motherhood far more than I imagined. My fears were based primarily on fantasies, she pointed out; the reality of my relationship with a child of my own would be radically different. I would not feel as confined, intruded upon, demanded from, and controlled as I thought I would. She was sure I was more adaptable than I gave myself credit for being. Why deprive myself of something wonderful based on unfounded, abstract, negative assumptions?

My response to her admonition and reassurance was a second train dream, where the only way I could change trains was to climb over a precipice, which two men were encouraging me to do. This dream told me that becoming a mother meant losing control and plunging into the unknown. Despite others' belief in me, it felt too dangerous to alter the "track" my life was on.

At this point I understood what I was telling myself and had a revelation, which I noted in my diary:

> I have finally accepted something essential: I don't want to *have* a baby—I just want to *want* to. I suspect that the reality has little to do with it, and my childhood a great deal.

23

Even though I passionately wanted this not to be so, my resistance had not dissipated or changed appreciably during years of self-examination. Instead, I saw how persistent, compelling, and profound it was on a visceral level, which I could not deny or alter by fiat. I had been ever-vigilant for the deep change of heart that never came, the requisite sense of longing for an actual baby, not just a feeling about myself. I had satisfied myself that I could deal with the anxiety if I really wanted to, but the enthusiasm needed to counterbalance my doubts did not materialize. It's difficult to distinguish between a fear that should be overcome, a challenge to change and grow, and one that must be heeded because it reflects something fundamental. This was clearly one of the latter variety. I didn't like it, but I couldn't ignore my own reality.

Then in a dream an Indian woman (representing traditional femininity) asked me when I would have "beautiful babies," and I, now white-haired with age, calmly replied "I don't want to have children." I'd finally stopped fighting myself. I had decided.

What I had really been doing all those years was less resolving a conflict than slowly facing aspects of myself that were contrary to my ideal and other people's expectations. I saw that in a significant way I was different from many other women, and from my own mother. I became most truly myself, warts and all, when I said "no" aloud. This was a "no" of affirmation, not just a repudiation of one kind of life, but the taking up of another.

Now that I had moved beyond motherhood, I had the task of creating a sense of feminine identity on my alternative "track." A final train dream showed the way:

I tried to get on a train with a student of mine who has two teenagers, but I discovered that she was already on board another one going in the opposite direction. I had to travel alone. "This train may take me to an inconvenient stop," I consoled myself, "but I know the way home; I won't be lost."

In the rush I'd lost my tote bag and purse. Although a man retrieved my tote bag, he hadn't found my purse. I was relieved to discover that it had actually been inside the bag all along. Once I saw it, I had everything I needed—my passport, my money, and my driver's license.

This concluding train dream resolves the themes of the previous ones. I end up on the train without the mother because I have to make the journey into childlessness, my new feminine identity, without her guidance or companionship. Though it may be an inconvenient and solitary way to travel, I can find my way now.

Losing my purse and tote bag, classic symbols for the female body, implies that I'm still afraid I can't feel like a complete woman without being a mother. A man returns my tote bag, the external manifestation of femininity; I'm still a woman in his eyes. But since my true sense of femininity must come from within, I have to recover my purse for myself. Through the decision process I've regained a full sense of womanliness and I'm ready to continue my life's journey.

2.

My decision never to bear children reflects my entire history, that interaction of temperament and circumstance, fear and desire, capacities and limitations, that makes me who I am. What seemed so aversive and alien in my vision of a child's demands was actually extremely familiar; the sense of entrapment in another's emotional needs and requirements for attention, regardless of what I was involved in, was the way I felt growing up, with my mother playing the part I ascribed to the baby I anticipated having. My father, too, contributed in his own more subtle way, as did my parents' relationship with each other.

My mother's loving control, her combination of admiration, inspiration, and imposition, started at my birth at the latest. She named me "Gene," on the theory that masculine names for girls were piquantly feminine. Since I was destined to become a writer, she explained years later, with the sort of logic that seems odd only when you think about it, she was conveniently equipping me with a prefabricated nom de plume, like the Georges Sand and Eliot. I was to be a woman who makes it in a man's world. It never occurred to her that I would want to pick my own monicker—or none at all—and might not even feel a need to conceal my sex, even if I pursued the profession chosen for me. My father stepped in and suggested that his daughter might prefer a girl's name, so I became "Jeanne," but my birth certificate was never officially changed.

I grew up in the suburbs of Cincinnati, Ohio. My father was a shy, serious anesthesiologist, and my mother an intense, flamboyant woman who had turned down a scholarship to study voice to marry him. Since doctors' wives didn't work, she devoted her talents to me and became the consummate fifties-style "homemaker." She suppressed any ambivalence or regret she may have had about her life choices; the only hint of rue was her chronic exhortation that I should always be able to support myself.

I don't recall my mother ever being sick, or even tired.

Her energy level was always remarkable—she could still exhaust me walking around a museum when she was seventy-five and continued to lift weights and swim daily at eighty-two—and she had charm, flair, and a generosity of spirit that impressed and fascinated, as well as an authoritativeness I found daunting. Her frustration with what she considered the provincial conservatism of her midwestern home was annually assuaged by a family pilgrimage to New York City.

Along with so much else, I inherited her love of Manhattan, where I have lived since I was twenty-one. My life here has been a source of pride and satisfaction for her, but at the same time she could not escape feeling, though she never directly communicated it, that I had abandoned her by deciding to pursue life—economically independent, as instructed—far from her. When I was a child, in awe of her vivid and compelling presence, I never saw that my mother was actually dependent on me.

Up to a point she nurtured in me a powerful sense of going my own way, even if she didn't always like the consequences. From birth, she liked to tell me, I had had a "determined jaw" and was so strong-willed that I turned myself over the day she brought me home from the hospital because I didn't like being placed on my back. Her conflicted admiration of what she interpreted as my assertiveness fostered my capacity to think for myself, even when I felt guilty or injurious in doing so.

My mother's unconscious plan for me, in addition to the career she had selected, was that I be her alter ego, and in many ways I fulfilled her desire. We resemble each other in our physical presence to such a degree that when we flanked a friend of hers in a dance class, the woman told me she felt like she was standing between mirror images. I share her taste, her practicality, and her self-righteousness. To perpetuate and also to limit our tie has been my lifelong project.

My father and I had a very different connection. He was the one who bestowed not only the name I've always gone by, but also my nickname, with accompanying nonsense songs, which he alone called me until it was revived by my husband. I was his "Jeanne Cat," the adored and adoring audience for the nightly tales he spun about the adventures of a bear and a princess, the diminutive child who delighted him by walking under the table and whom he told he gave special pills to keep her small. I was also his intellectual heir, who from the age of five accompanied him on his nightly rounds at the hospital, where he introduced me to patients and staff as "my assistant." I admired his calm competence in a crisis, his power to heal, his hands that could soothe any pain away. I tried to transfer his gift from the physical to the mental realm when I became the second Dr. Safer.

The idyllic communion with my father was never unadulterated and did not last. His long hours, as well as his discomfort with conflict and his wish to be taken care of himself, left my mother to cope, virtually single-handedly, with the less fetching aspects of child-rearing. It was always she who got up to give me bottles and relieve my nightmares in the middle of the night and who waited indulgently while I changed outfits five times in the mornings before kindergarten. My power struggles were all with her.

My father had trouble relating to an adult woman; he tended to withdraw, to avoid the intense engagement my mother required. He lavished his attention on me only until I, too, needed more from him than he was comfortable with, and she turned to me for what he failed to provide. Although he did champion me in my bitter struggle for independence from her in adolescence, he became increasingly remote from both of us. His battles with a variety of life-threatening illnesses exacerbated his isolation and emotional detachment, until by the end of his life I felt I hardly knew him.

It was from my own early experience that I derived the notion of children's omnipresence in a marriage, the saturation level of involvement required of mothers, and the conviction that conjugal intimacy is fatally disrupted by family life. My parents took me everywhere from the time I was six weeks of age, when I accompanied them on a trip to Quebec, because my father was afraid to leave me with strangers. My mother reminisced with pride intermingled with protest about washing out bottles by the hour even on the road and informed me that she had made my baby food herself rather than buy the inferior commercial variety. As I grew older, I was given lessons in everything, and my mother always drove me. Even in those days, when the division of parental labor was more skewed than it now is, she did more than her share; why did she never object?

Since I was the focus of my parents' mutual and individual devotion, it didn't register with me that I was an obstacle to their intimacy that they had both erected. If my mother felt slighted or rivalrous, she never expressed it, any more than I acknowledged my inevitable competition with her. Only in adolescence did I become aware of the tensions in my parents' relationship that drove them to the brink of divorce. When, to my shock, the fault lines of everything that had been suppressed between them finally yawned, my mother expected me to side with her.

Many women seek to recapture their childhoods by having children. For me to do so would have revoked one of the most stimulating parts of mine and revived one of the most problematic. My role as my parents' companion made me precociously at home in the world of adults, a position that, while I gloried in it, made me feel somewhat alienated from the "ordinary" world of children. While I had friends my own age, the sophistication and power of being a grown-up always beckoned, perhaps as an image of inviolable independence. In my hurry, I refused to have baby-sitters after age eight and often participated in my parents' parties, chatting with their guests until the early hours of the morning, which was the time I liked to go to bed anyway. I must have been afraid of losing this exalted status by acting too "childish"—awkward or whiny or sullen or stubborn— and consequently these traits became anathema to me. I have long since learned to be more tolerant of such natural feelings in myself, but I didn't relish reviving the anxiety or reliving the behavior with a child, either by identifying with it or having to put up with it as a parent myself.

Above all, I aspired to my own notion of maturity, which never seemed to include maternity. When I played with dolls, my role was the set designer or the stage director, not the mother. I had gotten the message that my mother's unconsummated talent was the real thing to emulate.

As an adult, I wanted to reproduce and enhance the special, ephemeral early bond between my father and me with my husband, to have the kind of union with a man that my mother had not had, and I must have concluded that being the kind of mother my mother had been—doing what he expected of her and what she expected of herself—prevented it. I knew that I could never be as dedicated as she without feeling deprived.

My mother was an impossible act to follow. Even though I intuited her mixed feelings and came to understand that for her own reasons she needed to do it all, I couldn't match her and would have felt compelled to try. For all her panache and worldliness—she certainly didn't look or act like the "maternal" type—being a wife and mother was the foundation of her identity, her principal source of self-esteem. Her perfectionism dictated that she be the impeccable housekeeper of a house with gleaming white floors, a fine cook, and ever-available for her family. It also required that I be the daughter who justified her heroic efforts.

The price of my mother's total devotion was my fidelity. As a result, I never felt that my emotional life was entirely my own. I always had to consider her and, if I didn't, deal with the consequences in our relationship or in my feelings about myself—I became selfish, ungrateful, even cruel, in both our eyes.

The only way to relate to my mother was to be part of her. I was the bearer of her destiny, the meaning of her life. Being the reciprocal center of each other's universe meant that going my own way, when it was irrelevant or opposed to her wishes, could only register as abandonment or betrayal. No other allegiance could be countenanced; she once accused me, with real pain, of preferring my friends to her. Remarkably, she adored my husband. He was the first man in my life she wholeheartedly approved of, and I had to admit that once again she was right.

As long as I stayed within my mother's orbit, as sure and silent as gravity, I could do and be anything I wanted. My individuality was her proudest creation, though it flourished in an atmosphere of almost imperceptible constraint. My fundamental needs were of necessity in conflict with hers, so that along with all the gifts for living that I received from her came an extreme sensitivity to intrusion, virtually instinctive now.

My sensitivity to all kinds of stimuli—noise, odors, other people's emotional states—magnified my psychological reactivity. This made the unremitting empathy my mother required both reflexive and aversive for me; I couldn't help it, and it was more than I could handle. There was nothing voluntary about the way I resonated with her, and there was no exit.

When I eventually disentangled myself from having to respond to her expectations, I came to understand that, no matter how I tried to the contrary, having a baby would propel me back to that world. Motherhood would automatically undo my hard-won separation from the woman who represented both the idealized mother whose devotion I could never match and the child whose presence I could never escape. In the context of my experience, becoming a mother myself could only mean subverting my precious, finally unfettered, will for the rest of my life—a thing that many women take for granted. By its very nature, the new mother/child dyad would recapitulate the old one.

I believe—and I spend most of my waking hours helping others realize—that a woman is not doomed to repeat her mother's life or her own childhood and that parents are not to blame for one's fate. My parents' love for me was never in doubt; the pain they inflicted was never intentional, and their lapses were a result of their own histories and struggles, of which I was only a part. I also know that family relationships have effects that cannot always be undone. Because of who I am and the dynamics of my family, I have had to forgo certain experiences in order to assure that I have what I need most. This means that things others tolerate I do not, that I would be too bothered by the constant arrangements and impingements, by the responses demanded by a child— things that would be less disruptive had I had a different past. Realizing this involved accepting my needs, my character, the integrity of my life, and my parents, in all our fallible humanity.

3.

On my fortieth birthday, my mother sent me my baby bracelet and the tattered hospital information sheet she was given the day before I acquired my pen name— when I was "Girl Safer, 7 lb. 8 oz."—and enclosed a tender note: "My dearest—some mementos of the day you were born. I've kept them all this time. Much love and many kisses." I wept, because I will never have a daughter whose infancy I will cherish and fondly remind her of years later. She kept every letter I ever wrote her, every present and painting I made. As much as I chafed under the burden, I was her achievement. I hate to disappoint her, and I hate to miss what we had, even though I know I must.

I am sorry to deprive her of the opportunity to lavish her love and inspiration on a grandchild. It would have brought out the best in her. And I'm sorry we cannot share motherhood; it would have been another bond between us.

My mother and I discussed children only once, briefly and awkwardly. "I guess your career is more important," she said, wanting to give me the rationale that I quickly grasped. There is of course some truth to that, but only some. Though my relationship with her resonated throughout the decision process, the real reason is the combination of factors that makes me require a certain freedom from constraint as essential for my well-being. Who we are together makes this inevitable. It is not her fault, or mine, or anybody's.

The way for me to assert my individuality as an adult

as I never could completely as a child was not to be a mother. Because it is my conscious, determined choice, it is an action, not just a reaction, an expression of who I am, not a rebellion against someone else.

It is precisely because I am so close to my mother in the way that I am that I found it essential to go a fundamentally different route. Choosing childlessness does not destroy our tie; it directs it into selected, suitable channels. Her stamp is on me emotionally as much as physically, and I am glad it is, because she caught me by example how to be vibrantly alive, to laugh, to love beauty, to know intimacy, and she did her ultimate to help me fulfill the promise she foresaw in that determined jaw.

Still, there is no denying that childlessness also implies ultimate separation and severs a basic identification with my mother, which many daughters conceal or compensate for by shared maternity. Every daughter and every mother disappoint each other in some significant way. Maturity requires that I see my decision as an autonomous act, independent of either meeting or thwarting maternal expectations, for which I alone accept the consequences.

Many people gain maturity by becoming parents, but I hope to achieve it by choosing not to. This demands self-reliance; having no one to live through or to do what you could not, forces you to seek meaning within yourself alone. I know everything depends on me. It really does for everybody, but children can permit parents to elude this essential and disturbing awareness temporarily.

Deciding against motherhood taught me truths I could have learned no other way. Acceptance of myself brought acceptance of my mother, along with a modicum of freedom from resentment and blame. The process has helped me to know and to embrace my own life and has expanded my awareness and compassion.

My diary entry for my forty-first birthday struck a decidedly different, more positive note than had my entry six years earlier:

> I want to record today that I looked in the mirror when I got up this morning and, despite everything, I did not dislike what I saw. It is an interesting face that is reflected. I feel hopeful (no easy thing for me) that Rick accepts me and that our life can be what we make it without a child.

Sometime later, when I reflected on the experience I had been through, I had a dream that explained the psychological meaning of childlessness to me so clearly that it needed no interpretation—a sure sign of resolution. In it, a friend told me, "When I'm afraid of doing something, having a child inspires me to do what I would never have been able to do, to cross the abyss for her." I replied, "What inspires me and spurs me on is that it's me—that it's *only* me. That's what makes me feel brave; that is my real accomplishment."

Here was the conclusion of the inner dialogue I had conducted, the ultimate validation from within of my own path. I knew where I stood and why.

4.

There was a totally unexpected result of my coming to terms, which I only realized had been quietly growing within me when it appeared; I began, quite naturally and almost unconsciously, to write. I'd published papers previously, mostly research and book reviews in professional journals, but now I found myself writing articles describing personal experiences for a general audience, in my own voice—and my own name. True maturity, I discovered, is doing something even though your mother wants you to.

This new direction was not intentionally compensatory. I never thought, "'I didn't have a baby, so I have to do something else"; opportunities simply presented themselves spontaneously. And to my amazement and delight, the very first attempt, a piece about my adventure designing and buying a belly-dance costume in Istanbul, was accepted for publication. To celebrate, I gave my debut performance (I'd been studying Middle Eastern dancing for ten years but hadn't had the courage before) in my teacher's studio, resplendent in my imported copper and black regalia. Working through feelings about motherhood had unleashed hidden reserves of creativity and femininity, and I emerged liberated, energized, and strong.

The article that meant the most to me was the one I wrote about why I was childless. Only after it was published and I found myself crying over the finality and concreteness of the printed words did I know that I had completed the process.

A wonderful dream—the last I had about motherhood—showed me how my experience of myself had been transformed:

> I was surprised and thrilled to find a vegetable garden, with a restored fountain and cantaloupes on the vine, growing on my parents' property in the dead of winter.

This dream complements the leafless, bird-filled trees of my very first motherhood dream. The cantaloupe was myself, the fruit of my parents' loins, which, though barren in the biological sense, was ripening out of season. This was my new definition of fertility, now organic and integrated. The restored fountain was the living water of my being, flowing beyond the childbearing years, ever replenished.

As soon as I fully accepted my position, I found myself starting to mourn for the possibilities I had lost by not having children. The satisfactions of my life and my new creative fulfillment consoled me but could not insulate me from feeling grief over the consequences of my action, right and healthy though it was.

There is no denying the precious things I gave up because of the choice I made. I will never see that complete trust, the delight of discovery, the unfolding of a personality I have helped shape and which will carry on some of my essence. I will never know what it feels like to have my child fall asleep in my arms or crawl into bed between my husband and me, as I used to do with my parents. Our love for each other will never be manifested in a human being.

Because of my choice, Rick's life has gone in a direction that would not necessarily have been the one he would have preferred. He told me recently about his own sense of loss, which he fully acknowledged only after the fact. In that understated way of his, without bitterness or accusation but full of feeling, he said, "I just saw one of the reasons people have children. A car pulled up in front of an office building to pick up a man after work. His wife was driving and his daughter was in the backseat, ecstatically calling, 'Daddy, Daddy!' when he appeared, as if he was the most important thing in the world." Rick was telling me that even though it is not essential to him, he misses being the center of a child's universe, as are his friends, his colleagues, and his own brother.

I remember how I used to look forward to the sound of my father's car in the garage when I was the child waiting and my father was the age Rick is now, my delight when he hugged me and sat me on his lap, and I realized how much it must have meant to him to find me at the top of the basement stairs. Any little girl would be thrilled to greet the kind of daddy Rick would have been. She would also be incredibly fortunate to have a father so full of love, so charming, and so wise, one who not only would draw cartoons, compose and perform songs for her, and listen with boundless patience and appreciation, but who would never abandon her, who would sustain her forever. I know I can't duplicate that experience for my husband with my greetings, however enthusiastic—no adult can or should adore like that. I feel sorry that he is missing fatherhood, which he would have loved, because of his love for me.

Neither one of us will ever reexperience wonder through our child's eyes. A friend told me about her four-year-old saying, untaught, "God is everything—this table, this tree." I envied another friend being able to explain the constellations to her enthralled daughter. I love helping people come into their own and express themselves, providing them with the security to develop, and I will have only an attenuated form of that kind of giving. When I hear patients or friends talk about their children, I know I will never have their experience, their delight in the unique connection. One part of life and love is closed to me; the closest I'll ever come was hearing the exaltation in a patient's voice when he called from the delivery room to tell me I was an "aunt," and knowing he would be a better father because of me.

I still struggle to accept as valid and sufficient alternative ways of nurturing outside the literal maternal role—the relationships with my husband, my friends, my students, my patients, one of whom told me recently, "you're my mother and father, teaching me the lessons of life." I miss the direct, immediate, continual experience even though I know how relieved I am that all but one of the people I love lives someplace else. There may come a time when I need to be special to a child, and it comforts me to know that I will have the opportunity with the children of my friends. "I'm glad that you'll be around when she's a teenager and won't talk to me," one told me recently. The weddings I will attend, the babies I will meet, will be theirs.

At the end of her final session, before saying good-bye to me, a patient told me out of the blue that she wished I would have a baby and take pleasure in that, as she knew I could. We had never discussed it before. I was moved and grateful because she was saying I had been a good mother to her and could have been to my own child, and she spoke with the authority of experience.

Sometimes it still seems strange, even presumptuous, when patients ask me for advice about raising their children. I am always gratified when they say it helps, that I understand and empathize with both sides. But I know I have a limitation because I have not had firsthand experience of parenthood, that I must extrapolate from my own memories.

Making a will, as I did recently, with no one to leave your possessions to, is a graphic reminder of mortality. What do I do with my jewelry? Parents never have to think about such questions—the answers are automatic unless something has gone seriously awry. There is joy and comfort in inheriting treasures, and in passing them on. I cherish the heirlooms that connect me to my family's past, and I will have no similar connection to the future.

Rick's reaction is a masculine variation of the same

feeling. He told me that he regretted that his unusual sur-name would not be carried on. Since his brother has two daughters, he said, the number of Brookhisers in the world would be reduced in the next generation. I knew this meant he was sorry not to have a son and heir.

One way Rick has found to work out his feelings about fatherhood—which he realized only after he had begun the project—was to write a book about why George Washington was the most successful founder of a coun-try in modern history. Washington, a man he deeply admires and believes is not sufficiently appreciated or adequately understood, possessed extraordinary paternal qualities. And, significantly, "The Father of His Coun-try" had no children of his own.

As for me, not only will I be nobody's mother—I'll be nobody's grandmother. I am not only the second Dr. Safer; I'm the last. Any wisdom I acquire cannot be passed down the way only a parent's can. My life, my world, everything I value (except what I have imparted through therapy or writing) ends with me. I will never have as direct an impact on anyone as every parent has on a child; my patients, if I do my job right, go their own way. Without the rationalization or the consolation of a biological legacy, whatever I achieve is solely my responsibility and painfully finite.

Childlessness has forced me to face existential ques-tions; a psychological bequest is real, but is never as palpable or literal as a genetic one. What gives most people a feeling of immortality or at least continuity will not be mine. I grieve that my parents' legacy, all Rick's gifts, everything we have to offer, will not be passed on. No one we know may want the collection of kilims we've gathered from our travels, the exotic tapestries that glint on our walls with their embroidered mirrors, or my antique kimonos. I can leave these things to causes I believe in and people I love or their children, but to no one who is part of me the way a child would have been. I will not impart directly the way I think, my taste, the joy I take in movement, in flowers, in talking, and I wish I could.

Since Rick and I have no relatives close by, almost all our holidays are spent warmly and happily but with other people's families. We have rare intimacy, at a price. These are the only times I really continue to feel like an outsider—even though I know my life fits me.

I went to a suburban health club recently where, to judge from the conversations I overheard, all the other women were mothers, and I realized just how unusual my situation was, but also how much it suited me and how lucky I was to be able to create it. I didn't feel defective, although I certainly felt different. I was grateful that I lived in a place where there was room for individuality, and that I had friends who had made the same choice to share my world, as well as friends who had children who included me in theirs.

It's important for me to remember that I am childless by choice, not by default. This gives me a sense of pride and self-acceptance even as I acknowledge what I am missing.

An old friend my age, who now lives in another state, just called to give me the specs on her newborn, delivered nine months to the day after her wedding, delight in her tired voice: "He has his father's chin, my nose, hair like both of us," she enumerated. Did I feel equanimity? No—I felt uncomfortable that I couldn't be as unambivalently overjoyed as she was, that I felt alien from her experience, even though I was pleased that she had what she had always wanted. I felt it made us more different, and because she's a peer—a noted scientist, artistically and musically talented, probably even more driven than I—I did momentarily feel like a loser in the Superwoman Sweepstakes. But compared with the anguish, the self-flagellation I would have felt five years ago, these were minor twinges. No issue as fundamental as this, as interwined with everything one is, is ever completely resolved without a trace. But, though I may occasionally feel inferior because I don't want what she has, I know I *do* want what I have. My world is rich and it is womanly. I hope I am becoming wiser and more complex with the passage of time and the deepening of experience. I see my ability to understand myself and to love others expanding, taking ever-surprising directions. I have chosen to have an empty womb, but I am creating a full life.

Part 2

Choosing a Childless Life:

Other Women's Voices

Chapter 1 →

Timetables:

When Women
Decide Against Motherhood

AFTER I DECIDED NOT TO HAVE A BABY, I WANTED TO KNOW
what the experience was like for other women who had
come to the same conclusion. When my friend Sandra
Singer read the article I wrote on the subject in 1989 for
the New York weekly *7 Days* and heard about my project
to interview other nonmothers, she volunteered to participate. "Finally a strike for our side!" this usually reserved woman exclaimed, echoing what I soon
discovered was a widespread reaction of relief and delight many of my subjects felt at discussing what had
often seemed to them—as it had at times to me—a
shameful secret they could share with no one. And it
was telling that, though Sandra and I had known each
other for years, until our interview she and I had never

shared confidences about this particular significant trait we knew we had in common. We discussed it as we canoed at dusk and picked pink water lilies on the little lake by her parents' summer place—the lake where she had spent every summer growing up and to which she is now the only one of her original playmates who returns without a family of her own.

Sandra views her minority status in her parents' community with a touch of irony but no bitterness; it is one of the few situations in which she feels like an outsider. "In my life," she told me, "not having children is perfectly acceptable since most of my circle of friends don't either—it's just at family gatherings that I feel different. I'm the only one there without a child, so they think of me as less than evolved. There's a certain hush when people say, 'she doesn't have children'—they always bring up a person they know who had a child in her late forties. People talk as if you have a fatal disease." She takes these reactions in her stride, aware that the life she has chosen can make other people uncomfortable and "interrupts the life cycle." But she appreciates what she considers its advantages and compensations. "It makes me sad to see parents who have wonderful relationships with their grown children, which I'll never know," she said. "Still," she added, "I realize how much my life has expanded."

Sandra Singer had had a premonition at the age of twenty-six that she would never be a mother, when she saw a baby who looked like the one she would have had if she had stayed with the boyfriend she'd just broken up with. If she hadn't decided to move to Chicago to go to art school and instead married the ambitious law student who wanted to settle down with a traditional wife and family, the diminutive but voluptuous Sandra, whose raven hair is almost as long as she is, would have been holding that baby boy with the dancing eyes and dark curls, rather than watching him wistfully from the next table at the restaurant. But if she had gone through with the marriage, she knew that she would have been the wife of a self-centered autocrat who would have thwarted the development of her artistic talents, much as her father had squelched her mother's. Sandra's mother actually had married her high school sweetheart, who became a professional ballroom dancer who wanted the spotlight eternally for himself, and she never picked up a paintbrush again. She became pregnant immediately and spent her life taking care of her family. "I never admired my mother's way of life," Sandra admitted. "My mother had many unrealized dreams, and I'm realizing them."

If things had gone differently, Sandra could well have been a mother herself—after all, she had dedicated her high school yearbook picture, "To my children: your mother was young once." Life offered her a number of opportunities to reconsider. And at several key points she did think it over again, most seriously at thirty-five, when she met Ibrahim, at the Middle Eastern nightclub in Chicago's Greektown where she occasionally moonlights as a belly dancer. He was a sensitive, intense Iranian engineer in urgent need of a green card. Ibrahim admired her talent, her determination, and her exotic flair and recognized an independent spirit similar to his own. Though she was very tempted to marry him, she declined because they had just met, and she knew his allegiance would always be with the large, traditional family he'd left behind. Although her own family was delighted with how her second career carried on her father's legacy, Ibrahim's would have been shocked if they had learned that she had ever danced professionally. The clash of cultures and religions, she was sure, would be intensified if they had a child.

Sandra had turned forty by the time Ibrahim was able to become a citizen and find a job in his field, and they moved in together. She had established herself as a photographer, and her priorities were clear. "The pressure was off by then," she recalls. "What I really wanted then was not to have a child—it was to have my first one-woman show," an ambition which she achieved that year.

Instead of having children, Sandra ended up making a career out of taking pictures primarily of them, without even knowing it. "Until an agent recently introduced me to a client as a 'photographer of women and children,' I never realized how many of my pictures are of children," Sandra reflects. "I know I have the capacity to touch the children I photograph; I see things for the first time through the child's eyes even though it's not mine."

Sandra now feels content with the choice she made. Passionately committed to her work, she can be found printing in her darkroom much of the time. Ibrahim is central to her, and she is deeply devoted to her friends, to her aging parents, whom she has nursed through various devastating illnesses, and to the motherless daughter of a friend of Ibrahim's, whose development into a startlingly lovely young woman she has tenderly documented in photographs. Sandra takes special pride that her protégée is now in art school.

As a result of her decision, Sandra channeled her creativity into art on a full-time basis and found alternative ways to fulfill her need to nurture. She believes that her childless state actually enhances her originality and artistic expressiveness. "Being an observer and a photographer requires a certain detachment," she explained.

"In order to be a sponge and keep looking at the world, I have to be unencumbered and experience things for the first time." Nonetheless, she knows that she has relinquished certain experiences even as she has gained others. Even though her life took a different course from what she anticipated, it feels right to her. "I've made my peace," she concluded.

As I met other childless women and read the research about them (which is not very extensive, since the phenomenon is only recently gaining attention), I discovered that many aspects of Sandra's story are typical: a slow, partly subliminal decision-making process, a dedication to her work, life circumstances (especially a mate) that make parenthood problematic, and a history that predisposes her to question, sooner or later, the virtually universal assumption women make that motherhood will naturally be a primary focus of their lives.

Sandra, like many women I spoke to, had been open to the idea of motherhood in the years before she eventually decided against it, and she gave it up only gradually. She even half-seriously reconsidered recently, in her mid-forties, when she saw an article about older mothers. As is common, she viewed her childlessness primarily positively, although she also experienced a sense of loss. She represents one end of the timing spectrum, the category of women whom researchers call "postponers" because they don't definitely choose childlessness (or like me, accept that they have already chosen it) until the end of their childbearing years. According to sociologists William Mosher and Christine Bachrach's article "Childlessness in the United States," in the *Journal of Family Issues* (December, 1982), two-thirds of all women who finally make this decision do it Sandra's way.

I eventually interviewed fifty women from all parts of the country, ranging in age from twenty-two to seventy-two, for this book. Each one had made a conscious decision not to have a family, with the exception of several of the youngest who were still ambivalent but leaning heavily in that direction. They had all been in a position to have children had they wanted to—there were men (usually husbands) in their lives, and there were no absolute medical contraindications or compelling external circumstances to prevent them. Though most were white, several were Asian, Hispanic, or black. Middle-class professionals from large cities predominated, but some lived in suburbs or small towns—including several who were the only childless women in their communities.

Like Sandra, quite a few had careers in the arts, but there were also secretaries, lawyers, nurses, and a lone housewife among them. A number of them had been in psychotherapy, sometimes for the purpose of resolving their feelings about maternity. And many described themselves as nonconformists, noting that they were the only siblings in their families not to reproduce and the only ones who had moved away from their place of birth. The age at which they made their decisions ranged from four to forty-five-plus.

This sample, though it is unscientific, nevertheless closely resembles the general population of voluntarily childless women in the United States, who comprise five to fifteen percent of American women, depending on how the statistics are calculated. Mosher and Bachrach cite studies that show that, like my subjects, these women are typically firstborn or only children, and that they are untraditional in a variety of ways. As a group they are better educated, more cosmopolitan, less religious, and much more likely to have professions than mothers are. Their most striking characteristic is that they have decided not to pursue the role that most women still automatically assume.

Sandra Singer's gradual route to childlessness was a common one among the women I spoke to; Tess Clark's was the diametric opposite. Her decision against motherhood was "early and absolute." "I decided not to be a mother at eight and never went back," asserted this vivacious redheaded choreographer in her Southern drawl. "It was always very clear; I've had no second thoughts."

Even when she was playing with dolls with her girlfriends in Memphis, Tennessee, she was adamant. "I clearly identified what my role was," she remembers. "I was the dancer or the choreographer, or a nurse because my father was so sick. The others were always the mommy. I used to say 'I'm *not* the mommy.' "

Tess had good reasons not to want to be the mommy, which had to do with how her own mother treated her and how she saw her mother's life. According to Tess, her mother had had children only at her husband's insistence, and mother and daughter—who was adored by her father and whose gifts he fostered—were outspoken rivals for his affection until he died, when Tess was eleven. "My mother disliked children, didn't want them, and let me know," she says, her voice still betraying a trace of bitterness, even though she has long ago mostly forgiven her mother, who has been dead for years. "She blamed me for my father's death, because he worked so hard for my sake." After he died, her depressed mother became even more rejecting and neglectful, so Tess sought and found a series of mother surrogates who all happened to be childless. Her role models were the actress who taught her elocution and the drama coach who introduced her to the glamour and romance of the movies, and Tess credits them with saving her life psychologically. She emulated them by becoming a dancer and charismatic teacher herself.

Although it's hard to imagine a duplicate of her, Tess was meant to be twins; she was born with two complete sets of reproductive organs ("I certainly did enough for two girls," she confessed merrily). In each of the six operations she underwent through adolescence as a result, the doctors insisted on reconstructing her uterus to preserve her childbearing capacity—even over her strenuous objections. Although women often have the opposite problem and must fight to avoid unnecessary hysterectomies, in Tess's opinion a hysterectomy would have been the more humane and rational solution for her unique situation. The additional pain she endured, and the outrage she felt when her wishes were ignored, only strengthened her resolve and resistance.

By the time Tess turned eighteen, living in the same house with her mother had become unbearable, and she became engaged to and planned to elope with a man who seemed virtually a reincarnation of her father. The only problem with Dick, whom she still considers the love of her life thirty years later, was that he adored children and definitely wanted several of his own. Torn between passion for him and aversion for a life that would have been uncomfortably similar to her mother's, Tess ran away to New York and became a dancer on Broadway. "Breaking our engagement was the biggest test of my conviction about motherhood," she told me, her eyes still brightening when she talked about the man she felt she had to give up for what she needed even more.

Now based on the West Coast, the ebullient and peripatetic Tess teaches theater dance around the country and has choreographed numerous successful reviews.

Though she never married, she has had several long-term relationships with men. In her own enclave, she is unfazed by her untraditional situation but still feels somewhat estranged when she sees her family. "All my relations have children but me—it was unthinkable not to," she told me. "I didn't dare talk about it with any of them, and I've certainly felt a stigma at family events. But I find support and guidance through my friends, many of whom, because of my profession, happen to be gay men." She also thinks attitudes toward women like her have changed for the better. "Not having children is more acceptable now than it used to be. You're not an outcast if you present yourself as strong, not sad and pathetic and unfulfilled." With characteristic flamboyance, Tess celebrated her fortieth birthday with forty male admirers and plans to invite fifty to her upcoming fiftieth. My husband, who met her and was charmed, asked to be invited. As for her decision and its consequences, she has "no, no, no regrets."

Tess belongs to the group researchers call "early articulators," those women—about one third of all childless women—who categorically and unambivalently reject the maternal role early in life. Like Tess, they view motherhood totally negatively. To set themselves apart from mothers (starting with their own) is a crucial part of their identity. They have usually had antagonistic relationships with their own mothers and needed to separate emotionally from them in a radical way; to consider motherhood would unconsciously keep them connected and identified with the embodiment of their childhood pain. Some of them even feel so strongly that they have themselves sterilized, actively excising any potential for maternity. Marriage for women like Tess is contingent on the prospective husband's agreement not to have a family and is often an important part of their bond. As

Janet Frank, another woman who claims to have been virtually "born knowing" she wanted no children and who also had a rejecting mother, put it, "One of the reasons I married my husband is that we each found somebody who didn't want a family."

"We opted for travel," summarized sixty-six-year-old Barbara Cowan, describing how she and her husband, John, had together determined—painlessly and implicitly, but quite definitely—that parenthood was not for them in their first years together, an unusual course of action in 1952. At twenty-six, the same age Sandra was when she eyed "her" baby in the restaurant but a generation earlier, Barbara had just married and set off for Paris with her new husband. There they enjoyed the bohemian expatriate life for two years while he researched his dissertation on French Indochina and she studied Southeast Asian art. Barbara made up her mind without deeply questioning why, and her husband concurred; when it was time to come back to the States, they realized without ever uttering a word that they didn't want a family, and John got a vasectomy. "Our decision not to have children was made then on some level," Barbara reminisced to me forty years later in her Oriental-accented apartment in Boston. "We never had to sit down and talk about it."

John became a history professor, and Barbara parlayed her artistic interests into a career as a representative for Asian artists. Their wanderlust continued unabated, and they vowed to spend at least three months abroad annually. Over the years they've lived in places such as Seoul and Bangkok and were off to Lisbon after we met.

The Cowans made their decision at a time when being childless by choice is even rarer than it now is, and Barbara has never regretted it.

She told me that she's proud to serve as a model for younger women facing the motherhood dilemma and reassures them that they, like she, can feel feminine and fulfilled without children. "I think of John and me as a complete family," she asserted. Her sense of satisfaction in life comes from having been instrumental in introducing to the West the work of many gifted Asian artists and from her knowledge that she has encouraged their talents and experienced their cultures in an immediate and intensive way that few outsiders ever can.

Sandra, Tess, and Barbara have all, in their own distinctive styles and following their own emotional timetables, made their decisions and lived with them for years. But the motherhood dilemma is a very live issue right now for Simonetta Fracci, a thirty-two-year-old playwright who gave me an eloquent account of her ongoing attempt to figure out what to do.

Lithe, honey-haired Simonetta is struggling to make it in a profession as male-dominated as the construction industry and far less lucrative. "People say you have to have a very big ego to succeed at writing plays, and I seem to have one," this soft-spoken, intense young woman told me laughingly. She's now had several staged readings of her work and is hoping to get her first professional production soon, but meanwhile she makes a living as a part-time copy editor. Her husband, Jake, is an actor who is frequently on the road. They have a tiny apartment in Brooklyn, no insurance, and completely erratic work schedules.

"For me the question is, do I want a child or do I think I want a child because everybody does? It's so ingrained. As I've watched the baby cards come in—the pictures of storks and all—I can't seem to really figure out what I want, and it makes me feel pretty weak. But the way I live my life—both financially and stylistically—I don't see it happening; my situation simply isn't conducive. I had a mother who was incredibly nurturing, and I have a great relationship, but I'm afraid a kid would tense things up and stress things out."

She waxed philosophical. "The thing about life is that everything feeds into everything else. If I decided to have a kid, I would have to change my entire life—structures would come tumbling down."

Simonetta is the youngest of four children of two Italian immigrants. Her father, an explorer and inventor, built the first Fiberglas boat. Though she admires both her parents, Simonetta had the distinct impression that family life stifled her father's creativity and increased his natural moodiness and frustration. Her mother, left to raise the children alone for long periods, was loving but controlling and developed no interests of her own. Although she's close to her family now ("I got all the rebellion out of the way" was her comment), Simonetta's adolescence was unusually stormy and left as a legacy "a stubborn, incredible love of freedom."

Simonetta had an addicting taste of that freedom when she came to New York as a graduate student. "Life really started then for me," she recollected. "I got deeply involved in writing and had two wonderful years competing with other students. I wanted to produce and really discovered myself. And I fell completely in love."

But the freedom to write is, as Simonetta sees it, in direct conflict with the requirements of family life. She knows that this isn't the case for every writer, but she fears it's true for her. "Although people say I have the perfect job for having a kid, I don't think it's true," she told me. She attributes part of her conflict to the pressure she feels to do and be everything—to play the roles of both her father and her mother. "This having it all thing is at the core—the sense that somewhere deep inside I do think I should do it all. To admit that I can't would be a defeat."

The anxieties that many of my subjects share haunt Simonetta. As she describes it, if she decides against motherhood, "I fear I wouldn't be a fulfilled woman, that I'd wake up at fifty and say 'You blew it.' But I go through entire days thinking of what I'm able to do because I don't have children. How could I write with kids in the other room? Can you really iron *and* write? What do you sacrifice as a result?"

Although she herself had devoted parents, she does not see much evidence of the joys of family life in the people that she knows—an experience childless women often describe, as though rationalizing a predilection of their own that makes them uneasy. "Everybody I know with children, their life looks bad to me," Simonetta said. "I wouldn't want that kind of life. They change their beliefs, they never have time for anything, and they're never really present. That puts a rebellious fire in me not to have children." And, like others facing the same decision, she contrasts the less popular position with what seems to her to be safe, comfortable, and conventional, though she views it with a slightly jaundiced eye: "But then sometimes I'm taken over with longing, wanting to plant flowers, stay home, and have children, with everything structured. Not doing it puts you in the category with the witches in *The Crucible,* into that other life that is so uncharted and mysterious."

So far, her dreams have alternative endings—either she's handed a baby and she's horrified or she embraces it with relief and delight.

One of the main reasons for Simonetta's reluctance to eschew parenthood is knowing what a wonderful father her husband Jake would make. Jake Donner is wry, direct, and extremely proud of his talented young wife. Theirs has been a joint decision-making process, each supporting the other and yet continuing to feel ambivalent.

"Since we got married so quickly, everybody assumed we had to, and they were confused when nothing happened," Jake told me. "Because of our ridiculous choice of occupations, we have no job security and spend tremendous quantities of time and energy on our careers. Now we have the flexibility to call the shots. I couldn't perceive having a child in our minuscule place with our financial situation. We're both so focused on what we're doing that it would be a strain on our relationship."

Since Jake is the only one of his siblings who married, he does get some pressure from his parents to provide grandchildren, but the real pressure he feels, like his wife's, comes from within. "I know in a way kids are a celebration of family and life, but if we had them, we'd have to stop doing what we were put on this planet to do."

Although statistically any couple childless after five years of marriage tends to stay that way, Simonetta and Jake are still struggling after ten, and struggling in a manner that ensures that they will make the right decision for themselves, whichever way they ultimately go.

"I choose never to be a mother" are hard words for many women to utter—it seems to be such a loaded statement, too final, like slamming a door shut. The minority who proclaim it readily, such as Tess, are a separate case, whose identity has long been contingent on repudiating the maternal role. Women like Barbara, who make up their minds early and easily, are unusual too; it is much more typical to experience a combination of avoidance, uncertainty, mixed feelings, and conflicting inclinations, as Sandra or Simonetta do. For them as for most women—myself included—motherhood is so fundamental to their notion of femininity that realigning their identity takes time to achieve, and until biology intervenes they hesitate to cut off the possibility.

Whether to have children is a genuine dilemma for a growing number of women, to be worked over for years, and reassessed periodically, as circumstances bring the issue to the forefront once again. It's not uncommon to rethink even what seems to be an ironclad position, either pro or con, at a critical moment, such as a birthday or a death in the family.

Gradual resolutions arrived at cumulatively and consolidated over time, like Sandra's and mine, predominated among the women I interviewed. The extended, complex, and not entirely conscious process reflects the natural anxiety that any responsible woman feels as she contemplates something as serious and central as motherhood.

Biology sets unavoidable limits on how many years a woman has to decide. How she deals with this imperative—whether she forecloses the possibility immediately, works it through methodically or sporadically, or drags it out endlessly—is a function of her personality and circumstances. Motherhood obviously has very different meanings for someone who rejects it at forty-four or four. The earlier a woman claims to have "known" she does not want children, the less distress she experiences about her choice, but she has cut something off thereby—that part of herself unavoidably connected to her internal relationship with her mother, however painful or problematic that may be. In contrast, the more central the concept of motherhood is to a woman's sense of identity, the longer it takes to give it up, and the more she needs an accumulation of "evidence," like

Simonetta's observations about the negative effects of parenthood.

Regardless of when it occurs, that change of heart and mind that leads to childlessness or the recognition that it has already implicitly taken place is, as I well know, a major emotional task.

Chapter 2

Moments of Truth

THOUGH NO SPECIFIC EXTERNAL INCIDENTS STAND OUT AS transforming moments of insight for me, many of the women I spoke with described such experiences. Their turning points took various forms. Some related how events as seemingly trivial as a conversation, or a fleeting thought or image, inexplicably lodged in their consciousness and came to epitomize a critical element that nudged them in the direction of childlessness—events whose significance sometimes only became clear when we discussed them. Others noted pivotal incidents, memories, or major life transition points—all of them dramatic, some of them extraordinary—that they defined as the nuclei around which their resolve took shape.

*　　*　　*

Few women face as striking a predicament over motherhood as Rachel Randolph did. This thirty-five-year-old journalist was living in Kashmir, where her husband was a cultural attaché, when it happened. Reporting on the Hindu-Muslim conflict there and researching a book on Islamic women, she had met many local families as she roamed the old section of Srinagar, the capital city, dressed in native garb, her blunt-cut sandy hair covered by a veil. One day an acquaintance of hers, a man whose family had made firearms for the local nobility for generations, strode into the American consulate with a three-month-old baby in his arms and asked to see her. "Take my youngest boy and give him a better life in America," he said, holding the lovely, lively child out to her. "He is the pride of my family. Raise him to be a good Muslim, or if that is impossible, a good Christian. You need a son—your life is not complete." His wife and his father enthusiastically supported this plan, he assured her. Moved by his plea and taken with the little boy, Rachel said she needed time to think it over.

Rachel had never imagined she would find herself reconsidering an issue she thought had been closed ten years earlier. When she and her husband had first married and she did not conceive, she had undergone eight months of fertility testing at his instigation. "In the middle of it, I found myself thinking 'Do I really want this?' and began wavering in my resolve. I got furious at Ray, because it had been his idea," Rachel recalled. Then they had made a mutual decision not to proceed. Was this offer compelling enough to make her change her mind and radically alter the circumstances of both their lives?

That she could be a good mother was never in doubt. Rachel doted on her nieces and understood children's perspectives well enough to think of writing books for them. She knew that she and Ray could give this little boy, so full of promise, opportunities he never could have without them; his shrewd father could not have found more suitable adoptive parents, immersed as they were in the child's own culture. But she wasn't ready to settle down, to stay put or go home, in order to provide the stability she believed he would require. To take on this child would mean returning to the kind of life that she had rejected, the kind that had made her own mother unhappy and frustrated. "My mother," she said, "was one of those women who should never have had children. She had a career as a retail buyer, but she left everything for my father and started having babies. She was furious as a young mother and never figured out why."

Rachel did not have the sort of job that could be pursued part-time; she had lived an unusually adventurous and somewhat perilous life as a war correspondent in the Muslim world, and her work thrilled her. "I like living my life as though I have nothing to lose," she explained. "I love the feeling that I'm willing to extend as far as I can without anything holding me back—that's the creative process. My opportunities wouldn't be the same with a family. Would I have gone into Afghanistan with the guerillas if I had a child at home waiting? It's a lot easier to do what I'm doing unencumbered." Besides, there were practical considerations: would she also be adopting an entire eternally extended clan of Kashmiri gunsmiths, who would someday all show up on her doorstep?

"It took me a month to decide against it, but it felt right on all levels not to," Rachel told me ten years later when she was in New York City promoting her latest book. "Still, the gesture was compelling. Fate seems to have thrust children into my arms."

This was, in fact, not the only time Rachel had narrowly escaped being given a child; she was offered several little girls in India on the same tour of duty. Each time, though she was sorely tempted and delighted by the children, she knew she had to decline, for, despite the Kashmiri's pronouncement, in her own eyes her life was indeed complete.

Several years after the incident in Kashmir, Rachel finally did come back to the United States and began to write novels for young readers about girls growing up in the Islamic societies she knew so well. Like Sandra Singer, the photographer, children occupy an essential place in her life through her work.

Rachel declined to raise someone else's baby; Tammy Lyons got an equally wrenching, opposite plea. "Have my baby for me," her best friend begged her from the hospital bed where she was recovering from the ectopic pregnancy that nearly killed her.

Tammy's friend Joan couldn't wait to have a family. They had been roommates when Tammy had moved to San Francisco from Tucson, Arizona, to become an art teacher and had stayed close. Tammy had been the maid of honor at Joan's wedding and the first person she had told when she got pregnant. And Tammy had waited anxiously with the family during the surgery that had been required to save Joan's life, comforting her afterward while she wept unconsolably. Now Joan was asking the twenty-five-year-old Tammy to be her surrogate—with Joan's husband as the father.

In her desperation, Joan could not think about the consequences of asking such a "favor"—and Tammy, because of her history, was more troubled about her own unwillingness to comply than by the enormity of the request. "It felt almost like my destiny to fulfill it," she explained. The daughter of an abusive, alcoholic mother and an ineffectual father, at an early age she had sought refuge with a community of nuns in Tucson, who became her surrogate family. "They saved my life," she told me, and she idolized them. She thought that, like them, she would never marry and have children but would instead join the order and "have the children of the world." The enlightened sisters recognized her talent, educated her on scholarship, and refused to let her join, encouraging her to pursue painting professionally. "They wouldn't let me ruin my life by hiding from the world," she remembered gratefully.

Although Tammy had followed their advice, she still retained remnants of her idealistic, devout girlhood, and so she guiltily pondered Joan's proposition. But, she asked herself, since she was relatively certain that she didn't want a baby of her own, how could she bear one and give it away, even as an act of compassion? Self-sacrifice was almost automatic for her, and yet she realized this could never work, either logistically or emotionally. Unfortunately, Joan was too involved in her own trauma to understand Tammy's point of view. "It ended our friendship," Tammy told me. Joan could not forgive her friend and never spoke to her again. Tammy was heartbroken, both because she had disappointed Joan and because Joan reacted so unfairly. However, she considered the experience a significant one in clarifying her own feelings.

Tammy was to rethink her decision several times after refusing Joan and even tried "borrowing" a child once, as many women who are uncertain about motherhood do, usually for the unconscious purpose of confirming their doubts. Now, married and in her late thirties, she is fairly certain that she has made up her mind.

* * *

Remarkable circumstances such as those that Rachel and Tammy dealt with certainly test a woman's resolve and force her to think about where she stands, but Pam Hall faced a situation more pressing because it was internal. Her problem was one of the most difficult that can befall a woman who is conflicted about motherhood: accidental pregnancy.

When Pam was in college, she had assumed she'd have a baby like everyone else she knew, and she had married "a guy who would have been a wonderful father—calm and nurturing." But things looked different to her when a year of student teaching showed her that she wasn't crazy about the idea. "I saw that I'd chosen my husband primarily as good father material," the rangy, stylish fifty-year-old literary agent told me. "I realized that he was dull, and I left."

Then at age thirty, only months into her second marriage, to a more compatible man, she found herself pregnant through a failure of birth control. Pam's response to this discovery was, as she reports it, strikingly rational and responsible. She was able to effectively suppress the pain most people would feel in such a situation: "I thought 'This is nice—if I wanted to be a mother, I could be, nothing is physically preventing me.' But I felt strongly that I wanted an abortion. So I went to a psychiatrist to be sure that I wasn't hiding anything from myself." Not only the psychiatrist, but also Pam's "iconoclastic" mother, gave her sympathetic support. "I was very lucky," she told me. "My mother said 'I don't need grandchildren.' I had no bad feelings and no regrets about it, although every once in a while I think that I might have had a twenty-year-old child now. The only thing I feel sad about occasionally is that I will never have the relationship with a child that my mother and I have. When I told my mother this, she said

'There's no guarantee that you would have. You can hope, but there's no correlation.' "

Pam's reaction to her abortion was unusually unambivalent; the other ten women I met who terminated pregnancies—some before it was legal and one two weeks before her wedding—mostly reacted with distress, transient depression, and a sense of loss of possibility, even though every one of them believes she did the right thing. Casting agent Myra Wyeth's account is typical: "In my brief second marriage, I got pregnant almost immediately. Deciding not to have that child was the easiest decision of my life—my salary was minimal, I was walking out of a failed marriage, and there was no stability in my life. But I wasn't prepared for how great pregnancy would feel. When I was actually going through the abortion, it was wrenching. Part of me physically reacted and wanted to scream out 'Stop this! Stop this!'—even though I knew it was my choice and the right thing to do. Afterward I was very sad, partly because I thought he would have made a great father."

Robin Green's unplanned pregnancy was also an emotional crisis, but the real reason she never became a mother was because she knew that the man she had married should never be a father. "I opted for marriage instead of children," this pert secretary stated on her twentieth anniversary.

Robin had her abortion when she moved out of her boyfriend Jack's house into a studio apartment after their tumultuous eight-year relationship broke up. She described the ordeal as "the loneliest time in my life." She had had major doubts about motherhood before, but was still drawn to the idea even though the circumstances were all wrong. "This felt like my one chance to have a child," she recalled, "but I had nobody in my life. I had a severe reaction to the abortion and cried all weekend." The experience brought Robin and Jack back together, and they married not long afterward.

Having a family with Jack was out of the question. He was fifteen years older than Robin, from a radically different background (blue-collar Irish Catholic vs. her upper-middle-class Jewish), and he had a drinking problem. In addition, their child-rearing philosophies were irreconcilable. "We had entirely different notions of discipline," the laissez-faire Robin explained. "For him children had to abide by rules and regulations, and he would have been very strict"—just the kind of father she had rebelled against as a teenager. Through lots of mutual hard work and therapy, their relationship has prospered over the years, but the extra stress of children would have destroyed this carefully nurtured union. "If we'd had them, we'd be divorced by now," Robin said.

Living in suburban Long Island, Jack and Robin are the only couple they know without a family. Nonetheless, they manage to have children in their lives to the degree that suits them. Their house is full of other people's kids, and they have baby-sat for and befriended several generations of their friends' offspring. "What makes it nice for me in the suburbs is I have all the children nearby," Robin told me enthusiastically. "I'm able to share their growing up—it's accessible. Having them around keeps us young. The next-door neighbor's son has become 'our' child." Robin has virtually been the surrogate mother of this boy, who asked her to walk down the aisle with his immediate family at his wedding. It was the perfect compromise for her.

Like Robin, many women ostensibly make the decision to foreclose motherhood when they marry; even for the majority, who put off considering the whole topic when they were single, the question inevitably arises when a prospective father enters the picture. Curiously, though, couples rarely disagree on parenthood, probably because many of these women have been leaning away from motherhood all along and subliminally select men who either agree with them or with whom it would not be possible. Finding a mate who is too old (a more likely occurrence because many of them marry later in life), who has children already, or who is unsuitable, unwilling, or physically incapable of paternity removes the overt burden of choice. As Jane Michaels, a child psychiatrist who married a man dead set against a family, put it, "I've always been ambivalent about motherhood, even though I like children and specialize in treating them. Had there been a different man in my life, I might have had one, but I shut the door on that possibility by marrying a man who didn't want them. I had to ask how important it was to me. In retrospect, his stance probably made it easier."

Medical problems can force a woman to make up her mind about motherhood in a hurry. Should she try to have a baby before it is too late, despite her doubts? If infertility looms, how much time, effort, and money is she willing to expend trying to conceive? Does she want a baby enough to consider adoption? Sometimes her very hesitation to pursue parenthood at any price demonstrates that she is less deeply committed to the proposition than she thought she was. While she may have believed she wanted children (and on some level genuinely did), in retrospect she can admit she was glad she could not have any.

Such a crisis confronted Paula Holbrook at the age of thirty-six. Paula, a full-bodied blond with a serious, expressive manner, had in her twenties come to New York from a small Ohio town to become an actress and had discovered instead that directing was her métier. At thirty-two she married her mentor, a well-known theatrical producer many years her senior. Despite her own misgivings, he was willing for them to have a family together if she really wanted to, but Paula was uncertain because she knew that children would make her chosen profession—still an unusual one for a woman—more problematic. "In this business work is often last-minute, and sometimes being able to pick up and go out of town on no notice can be your break," she explained. She was weighing her options when she discovered, at thirty-six, that she had to have a hysterectomy. "When I needed the surgery, I knew that this was it," she told me. "I went through soul-searching. My gynecologist was wonderful and offered to try to reconstruct my uterus if I wanted to keep open the possibility, even though it would be risky. I had to face the fact and be realistic with myself. I realized that I knew I didn't want kids, that I never really had."

Even though she had no control over the necessity for surgery, Paula took control over the decision-making process. "At the time of the operation I told myself that this was my decision," she said with conviction. Not long afterward, her husband died suddenly. "Thank God I hadn't gone ahead and had one—imagine what it would have been like to be a widow with a child in my profession," she said as she reflected on the hardest time in her life.

Despite the grief she endured, Paula feels thankful for the way things turned out and proud of herself. "Not everything in life is the way you think it's going to be, and your life goes a certain way—if you go with that. Facing what I've faced has made me stronger. I've kept the core of myself. The way my life progressed has allowed me to keep my dream—I never gave up what's important to me, the theater, and I'm really starting to make it now." About her decision not to risk bearing a child, she says, "Maybe I have missed something there, but I just don't feel it."

It was nothing dramatic or traumatic—just a casual conversation with a woman who worked for her—that opened Jackie Fast's eyes to her real feelings about motherhood. The frank, freewheeling filmmaker was twenty-seven at the time and had hired a younger woman to help her renovate her apartment. "She was a single, twenty-two-year-old mother, pretty but obese, who was struggling to support herself and her hyperkinetic child," Jackie remembered. "We were having lunch one day, talking about children. I had just started to hit my stride in my career, and I said, 'I'm not going to have children until I'm making fifty thousand dollars a year so I can have full-time help and don't have to do anything for them.' She looked at me and said, 'If you don't want to take care of a child, why do you want to have one?' And I said, 'You're right.' She saw through all my bullshit."

Unlike Sandra Singer, who reconsidered the question several times when her circumstances changed and only gradually came to her conclusion, Jackie's exchange with her helper unambiguously convinced her of her own position.

Jackie, who proudly describes herself as a "black sheep" who "would rather die than conform," had done one highly traditional—and, to her continuing amazement, highly successful—thing in her life: at twenty-two she had married a like-minded screenwriter. Pete always opposed fatherhood, but Jackie had wanted to keep her options open until her illuminating exchange with her helper.

When she was thirty, Jackie's gynecologist asked her whether she was planning to have a family, and she had a response ready. "He asked me very thoughtfully whether I felt envy or sorrow for the pregnant women I saw in his waiting room, because that was a good test. It was so clear when I answered honestly."

Twenty years later, now that Jackie is comfortably exceeding the salary she had stipulated as her minimum to consider motherhood, she relishes her childless marriage and a freelance career tailor-made to her temperament. She spends much of her time scouting out exotic locations for films and directs documentaries on such topics as the Beat Generation. "I've never looked back or felt any conflict since I made my choice," she told me. "And I'm so lucky that Pete's so terrific and we fit so well."

Jackie's critical conversation occurred in her late twenties and influenced how she dealt with the issue of motherhood later in her life. For Charleston-born nurse Anita Stark, a dream she had at the age of forty provided confirmation of the course she had been pursuing covertly for years. Lively Anita is a freckled strawberry blond whose drawl got appreciably deeper when she was visiting me up North. She had ended her early first marriage, to a man who turned out to be mentally unstable, before she was able to get pregnant. "As the marriage started to disintegrate, I was very glad inside that we hadn't had any kids yet, because I couldn't have handled it alone, and I certainly wouldn't have wanted continual contact with him," she confessed. She was twenty-five when they divorced, and she picked up the pieces of her life by going back to college and eventually getting a graduate degree in nursing administration. Anita lived in several Southern cities over the next ten years, until she finally returned to her home town, where she became director of nursing at the general hospital.

Much of this time she was being courted from afar by

her old high-school sweetheart, but she didn't feel ready to risk remarriage until she was thirty-eight. "The baby question came up again then," she told me. "We talked it over—it wasn't too late. I was very relieved when Teddy said it would be fine with him either way—he had a daughter already—so there was no pressure. I searched my heart about it, and then I had a dream. I dreamt that my gynecologist came in and said, 'Anita, you're pregnant,' and I screamed 'No!'—like it was horrible. I woke up with tears running down my face, and I knew I didn't want to do it."

Anita's dream showed her how frightened she was about becoming a mother, and she felt no need to fight against her fear; at that point in her life she was more interested in making her new marriage work, in renovating the quaint old house on a lake they had bought, and in helping Teddy start a business producing and selling a new truck-loading device he had invented. Unlike Jackie, Anita does feel a sense of loss, but she puts it in perspective. "I do love my nieces and nephews, and I see how nice it would be to participate in the future," she acknowledged. "Sometimes I feel that I am personally missing something, but this is the way it is—the way I am—and I'm not unhappy about it."

People can turn either way at a turning point. Why did Rachel, Tammy, and the others make the decisions they did, when other women facing the same situations would have embraced motherhood, overcoming their fears and doubts? The same incidents would have a different meaning and radically different outcome for a woman inclined to motherhood.

The reason these key experiences and their reverberations had the effects they did is that they helped these women recognize and in some cases clarify internal tendencies they hadn't acknowledged before. Focal events are really the culmination and crystallization of a profound mental process.

The significance of their moments of truth lies in the fact that they revealed to these women something about themselves that caused them to question one of the basic tenets of our culture. The inner sources of this personal insight are to be found in their pasts and their personalities, in the combination of history, character, and experience rooted in early relationships, which shapes an individual's destiny in idiosyncratic and unpredictable ways.

A variety of factors make women psychologically receptive to considering the childless alternative, and then a combination of what happens to them and how they choose to live causes them ultimately to embrace it. As Rachel Randolph said after she refused to adopt the infant in Kashmir, "You make your own circumstances, but they also guide you into your next circumstances."

Chapter 3

The Wrong Stuff:
Personality Factors

As I was having lunch in a neighborhood café one day, a young woman walked in holding her little son's hand. I noticed she had dressed him in a delicious outfit—black and white jacket, baggy pleated black pants, topped off by a white hat with black points around the crown—an ensemble with the kind of panache he'd probably never dare to display again until he was ready to buy Armani for himself. "He just wants to walk up the steps. Is it okay?" she asked the obliging manager, with a mixture of indulgence and embarrassment.

For the next fifteen minutes, everyone in the restaurant watched this child as he methodically ascended and descended the staircase, testing his still-inconsistent coordination with determination and sublime self-absorption.

His mother sat patiently smiling at the foot of the stairs until he was ready to leave. That took another five minutes because she first had to dissuade him from gathering up as many apples as he could hold from the basket at the door.

When he had toddled out beside her, both of them pleased with the success of their expedition, I wondered how she was able to do this with such good grace on a regular basis. It was all very charming, I thought, but what if she'd been exhausted or preoccupied or just wanted to think her own thoughts? What if she was in the middle of an absorbing project? Why wasn't attending so single-mindedly to him a trial for *her?*

Like me, many of the women I talked to believed that they had "the wrong stuff" for motherhood. They, too, felt deficient in some of the key qualities that they and everybody else deem essentially "maternal": patience, tolerance for intrusion, and the ability to put oneself aside for prolonged periods without deep resentment or anger. They shared a belief that as mothers they could not maintain certain conditions necessary for their own well-being, such as privacy, uninterrupted time for self-development, and, most especially, freedom. These character traits and requirements caused some of them to question their femininity or worry about being selfish, as I had. On the other hand, others were insouciant or even defiant, reflecting a nonconforming spirit they'd had since their teens. Whatever their reactions—and no matter what other women felt—they agreed that they felt an irreconcilable conflict between taking care of themselves and meeting a child's needs; the satisfactions of child-rearing did not seem to offset the costs. Despite the fact that motherhood is supposed to be a woman's supreme fulfillment, for them it seemed more of an obstacle to fulfillment.

Sharing their physical and emotional space with a

child on a full-time basis feels more aversive than attractive to these women, and the noise children inevitably and quite naturally make epitomizes their fear of feeling intruded upon. They know that the decibel level of life automatically rises around even the best-behaved child. The nature of that noise is chronic, pervasive, and under only limited control. Parents must learn to endure assorted sonic bombardments ranging from crying to video games, tumultuous play, and countless renditions of the "Barney" song in their own homes. Unlike city dwellers contending with such external nuisances as ambulances, car alarms, or heavy-metal serenades from neighbors, parents cannot just tune out the racket; they have to keep one ear cocked.

It was a raucous weekend *en famille* that provided the final evidence for Jackie Fast that she was not cut out for parenthood. The incident occurred right around the time that the filmmaker had her telling conversation with her helper, which had showed her in the abstract that she didn't really want to take care of a child. Her husband had been against parenthood all along, but she hadn't definitely ruled it out until this weekend confirmed her conviction. "My husband and I were staying at our landlord's country house," she recalled. "They had seven-year-old twins, very rambunctious, who were running throughout the house. We knew this was normal. Pete and I were trying to sleep on Saturday morning, and the kids opened the door, squealed, and jumped onto the bed. I turned to him and said, 'You're right. I don't want any of these. Let's forget the whole issue.'" Her ears confirmed what her mind had already figured out.

Cindy Gardner, a forty-year-old nutritionist, has such a need for peace and quiet that she works two fifteen-hour days in Manhattan so that she can spend the rest of her time in her cozy little house with her six cats and her husband, Randy, in a bucolic corner of upstate New York. Cindy, a droll, petite blond who loves ethnic clothes and Southwestern jewelry, realizes that the style of life that suits her would not be compatible with children, much as she delights in them.

"I love calm and quiet—it's a big problem," she told me one night when we were having a slumber party because both of our husbands were away. "The noise would drive me nuts. I'd have to have a deaf-mute child who likes to read a lot and a very big place to live."

But children's noise is not solely an annoyance to Cindy; it is also a symbol of the vitality of family life, which she regretfully realizes runs too counter to her temperament to be comfortable for her. She knows she is giving something up. "My in-laws' homes are filled with life and joy, and I feel a little empty and sad sometimes; mine is quiet and still," she told me. "Something's missing—the warmth and laughter that goes along with having a family. I think that life is richer and fuller when you have one."

Cindy is no recluse. She meets friends for lunch, participates in professional associations, and sees every foreign movie that comes to town. She recognizes, though, that she needs long stretches of time alone to maintain her equilibrium and to keep from being overstimulated and exhausted by the pace of life in New York. When her husband, who designs accounting systems for small businesses, is out of town, Cindy relishes the tranquility of curling up in front of her fireplace for a few days with a novel and a selection of felines. Even though she and Randy are inseparable after fifteen years of marriage, they rarely eat dinner together during the week because of the discrepancy in their schedules. They both know he would make a terrific father, since he is patient and deeply understanding, but they've agreed that a family would be unfeasible. Instead, they have opted to be the favorite uncle and aunt of his brother's children.

Having been a latchkey child herself, Cindy believes it would be unfair to expect a child to conform to her kind of life—and even more unfair to expect herself to conform to a child's timetable. "I can't imagine sleeping on a child's schedule," she said. "I like to wake up when I'm ready to. I can't make it on a little sleep, and I hate even when my husband wakes me. It's a metaphor for regulating my own life, going at my own pace."

Sleeping on their own schedules symbolizes self-regulation to many childless women. It's not when they go to bed or get up, or even how much sleep they get, that matters most, but the fact that they're in control. As Nancy Sherman, who owns a Victorian inn with her husband in Mendocino, California, put it, "I like to be able to wake up in the morning and know that the day is my own, even if this sounds selfish."

Nancy's days are extremely hectic. She's rarely home before eight P.M., takes minimal time off, and she and her husband are on call around the clock—but she's chosen this life, and she loves it. So much responsibility leaves Nancy little time for herself, and she needs to use it in her own way, which includes daily meditation sessions and long hikes in the country. "I really need space and boundaries to maintain my inner balance," she explained. "An additional set of demands would overwhelm me."

Neither Cindy nor Nancy is free from obligations; they set alarm clocks and consult Filofaxes and have career and other responsibilities that subject them to considerable regimentation. What is it about a child specifically that feels so much more disruptive to them? Why can't they tolerate the conflict as do mothers, who, with varying degrees of success, seem to be able to integrate their child's requirements into their lives and to see those needs as extensions of their own? Attending to a child has a different psychological meaning for them, a meaning that derives from their personalities, their relationships, and their formative experiences. For childless women, getting up at six A.M. to teach a class, prepare for a meeting, or deal with a heating emergency isn't pleasant, but it feels like a qualitatively different kind of demand from being awoken at the same hour on a regular basis by a two-year-old who simply wakes up then. They also tend to gravitate to independent professions where they are usually free to create their own hours and working conditions. No matter how busy they are, they have what Simonetta Fracci, the young playwright, called "an incredible stubborn love of freedom."

Paradoxically, many of the women who prize and exercise freedom the most feel it could be easily jeopardized, especially by a child. Rachel Randolph, the roving journalist, told me, "'As I get older I value my independence even more. I'm fierce about maintaining it, and it's hard for me." Women who have worked hard to establish their autonomy—and who have had to overcome their own compliant tendencies or struggle to separate from intrusive or demanding mothers—see motherhood as a threat to their liberty. Because of their potential overinvolvement and difficulty setting limits, they're afraid that a child's requirements would compel them to give so much that they would give themselves away.

Jane Michaels, a former dancer who went to medical school in her late thirties and became a child psychiatrist, feared that her response to a child's demands would obliterate her hard-won identity. She frankly described the mixed feelings her sister's new baby aroused in her: "When I hold her, it's wonderful, but I'm also repulsed by this thing sucking off me. A child takes so much time and energy that I would be afraid of losing myself. I tend to be a loner, and I need to be. I worry whether I could give enough to a child—and if I would want to because of what it takes out of my life. My boundaries and my own needs would disappear." For women such as Rachel and Jane, childlessness is both a preference and a means of self-preservation.

The first thing many women who live through a trauma want to do as soon as they recover is have a baby, to underline and celebrate their survival. Eva Martinez had the opposite reaction; getting hit by a bus at the age of thirty made her want to concentrate on her own development more single-mindedly than she ever had before. A dark-eyed, gracious and ample woman, Eva still moves and speaks with some difficulty twelve years after suffering a brain concussion and having both legs shattered by the bus that careened into her as she was crossing a street. It took a year of rehabilitation for her to recover physically and mentally—during which time she fell in love with and married the doctor who saved her life. She spoke with a quiet intensity about topics she has strong opinions about but rarely feels comfortable discussing. "It's good to come out of the closet about this," she told me. "I've gone through so much emotional and physical pain in my life that I want no more. Most people don't understand or accept my position. They're not open, so I don't want to risk mentioning it, even woman-to-woman. I'm vulnerable when I talk about it, and I get angry and defensive. It's understood that women are supposed to have children and if you don't, there's something wrong with you. I was reared to have children and not to think of myself first, like the perfect mother in Virginia Woolf's *To the Light-*

house. Not to want to makes me selfish and means that I don't think about the future."

Despite her convictions, going against her family's expectations and Hispanic cultural tradition, which places so strong an emphasis on motherhood, was a struggle for Eva. "The decision was hard. Even my therapist questioned me, although my husband supported me completely. I felt like I was always justifying myself. I used to worry that I really was being selfish, but I've resolved that I come first. I need to be healthy most of all. I don't feel I'm missing out, but I'm still afraid that something's wrong with me because other women need to have kids and I don't."

Eva felt that she had put herself aside her whole life, and her accident made her passionately intent on doing so no longer. For her, having a child would have been a continuation of her past, when she never felt free to be herself because she had to meet other people's expectations and take care of them. Born in Connecticut of a light-skinned aristocratic mother and a lower-class black father who had both moved there from the Dominican Republic, Eva was "the token Hispanic" throughout her childhood. She was her mother's confidante and the focus of her mother's foiled aspirations. Her parents' marriage was unhappy, and when Eva was nine years old, her mother told her that she had a lover. "My parents stayed together for me, but I knew what was going on," she said. "I wouldn't want to do that to any kid." Eva did not want to recapitulate a situation in which a child would feel, as she did, that she was standing in the way of her mother's happiness.

It is a child's constant, unavoidable presence and chronic need for attention that Eva would find onerous. "A child is right there and does not go away," she explained. "You cannot ignore its needs. When women become mothers, often they don't even have one or two hours a day for themselves, and they have to plan it. You're expected to put yourself on hold as an individual. Why should I do that for the rest of my life?"

Despite her difficult family situation, Eva had positive experiences and relationships as a girl that showed her an alternative way to live. Her happiest memories were the summers she spent with two childless female cousins who became role models for her. "They had plantations near Santo Domingo, which they ran themselves," she remembered. "I loved and admired them—maybe that's why I became a horticulturist."

One of the first things Eva did after her recovery was to become an expert in historical gardens, which she now studies and designs. Last summer she traveled to Oxford University to study nineteenth-century gardens. "I couldn't have gone there if I had a child—it was hard enough for me to manage it alone," she said. Even though she knows she would not be able to do what they do, Eva admires and supports mothers who maintain their independence. "There was a woman from Sri Lanka who had left her family to take the course. I thought it was fantastic, but I saw how one of the women was trying to make her feel guilty because she had left her children behind, and I stopped her."

Eva refutes the notion that she has no commitment to the future because she chooses not to be a mother. "I want to do something for the next generation, and I'll do it without children of my own," she said with certainty. "I'll be involved in education for the rest of my life." The magnum opus that she is now researching and dreams of writing soon is a book on her favorite topic, the "sex life" of plants.

A woman such as Eva, whose temperament and history make her sensitive to intrusion and who feels she has never been able to be her own person, can experience children as an infringement and conclude that she's not right for the job. Such a woman implicitly contrasts her attitude with what she imagines a "good mother" would feel. Her notion is partly an idealization based on an internal image of who her mother was (or ought to have been), but it also has a foundation in external reality. The good mother, she imagines, accepts the disruptions and demands and makes meeting her child's needs her principal priority; moreover, she's happy to do it. She makes the commitment with an attitude of devotion and satisfaction. Gratification far outweighs any feelings of frustration, deprivation, anger, or resentment. Such a mother might not positively *enjoy* being interrupted on the toilet or while composing a symphony, but she would handle it with sufficient equanimity.

The need to be the center of their own attention, which Eva, Nancy and many others emphasize, is not selfish, as popular prejudice judges it to be. This desire is not based on narcissism, immaturity, or an inordinate need for adulation—traits that are, unfortunately, as common among mothers as nonmothers. Instead, it expresses a healthy wish to focus on their own lives, often for the first time. Cindy, who has just recently started publishing in her field and who has now completely shaken the bouts of depression that used to plague her when she was younger, explained, "I'm moving toward a more creative phase in my life: I'm becoming more myself. Having a child would put my own development on hold for years. I don't have children because it would take away so much that I'm just discovering in myself, that I have to discover alone." Diana Russo, a journalist, thinks that exploring her newfound self-expression as a novelist would have to detract from what she could give to a child. "I might shortchange a child by concentrating on my writing as I need to. I feel fortunate that I don't feel compelled or obliged to give up what's right for me."

Of all the attributes necessary for motherhood, patience is the one in which voluntarily childless women most often feel deficient, and they realize this would be a real liability in a situation where they would not be in full command and from which they would not have the luxury of walking away. Either the "good mother" they picture is more tolerant by nature than they or her relationship with her child inspires her to become so.

The voluntarily childless woman finds maternal responsibility almost claustrophobic. To her, a child makes demands merely by existing—and it has a right to a mother's undivided attention on a regular basis. As Nora Adams noted, "Being a mother means infinite patience and devotion to a little creature that needs you and deserves your time. That kid didn't ask to be born."

Raising a child is an unpredictable project in the long run, and this presents difficulties for women who like to be in charge. Jackie Fast concluded that the only legitimate way to write the script for someone else's life and guarantee the outcome—as so many parents try to do, with disastrous results—was to make movies. "A child hopefully leads its own life and goes off," she commented. "The beautiful thing about movies is that they stay the same; something I worked hard on continues to be what I want it to be. No one should feel that way about a child."

While the duties they specifically associate with motherhood seem oppressive to them, the nonmothers I met pride themselves on being generous, nurturing, and deeply committed people on their own terms. They see their brand of caretaking more as a choice than a handicap. Barbara Cowan, the Asian artists' agent, never wanted a family but loves to mother the artists she represents. "It's not about being responsible, because I take responsibility. I simply didn't want to make that specific kind of commitment."

They all make a distinction between parental duty and the kinds of duty they embrace. What they reject is being needed continuously and all-inclusively by someone whose very survival depends on them. Robin Green, the secretary who "opted for marriage instead of children" and who is nothing like the stereotype of the cold, detached, self-involved childless woman, summarized the difference: "I don't have to—mothers have to." Though Robin's need to avoid obligatory caretaking extends even to quadrupeds ("I don't even want a dog; I don't want anything or anybody to be responsible for other than myself"), she willingly spent years helping her husband fight alcoholism and is as devoted to her elderly boss as any daughter. For her, taking care of adults, no matter how needy they are, is not the same as taking care of children. Likewise, Tess Clark, the peripatetic choreographer, moved in to care for a gay friend with AIDS for three months and volunteers weekly in a nursing home, where she teaches the residents how to dance. "I spend innumerable hours with dying friends and old people—it's my way to nurture. I never run out of giving with them, but I'd be in a mental hospital if I had a kid," she exclaimed.

Since women who are childless by choice are typically perceived as self-indulgent and immature, it is striking how many of them cited their sense of responsibility as the factor that prevented them from becoming mothers. An "overdeveloped sense of duty" disqualified Linda Krystal, an actress who spent her thirties forging her career, for motherhood. "A child sets the demands," she said. "I'm limiting my burden of guilt by not having one." Anna Lincoln, an acupuncturist who had bummed around Asia in her youth, criticized the insouciance of the hippie mothers with barefoot babies she encountered in Kathmandu; she herself "would never do that to a child."

Total commitment to whatever they undertake matters a great deal of childless women; they reject parenthood, in part, because they lack the requisite "burning desire" that they bring to other major life enterprises. Many see themselves as perfectionists who could never live up to the impossibly high standards they would impose on themselves. "My parents were very involved, which makes me appreciate that to do it right requires incredible commitment, for which I'm not prepared," said Janet Frank, a corporate lawyer. "It would mean so much time and self-sacrifice. I couldn't duplicate their dedication." Like photographer Sandra Singer, many of them had mothers who were always home to feed them lunch, who fitted their lives around their children, and they feel they should be willing to do the same. "I had a full-time mother, and I would want to give one hundred percent like she did," Sandra said. "Since I can't, it's not the right decision for me." Michiko Nicholson, a textile designer, echoed Sandra's sentiments. "My foster mother's devotion and selflessness would have been a very hard act to follow." These women know that a life so oriented to another person would not make them happy, and they don't want to enter a competition with their own mothers when they know they would lose.

They also don't want to risk imposing their unrealistic expectations and exacting standards on a child, as many of their own parents did. Nancy Sherman assessed herself candidly. "My personality isn't all that tolerant. Accepting flaws wouldn't be easy. I'd be too demanding and rejecting, and I wouldn't want to pass that stuff on."

Personal freedom—what Nancy defined as "doing what I want when I want"—is central to all the women I spoke with, and avoiding the intrusion and constraint that caring for a baby entails is an essential component of their particular brand of freedom. Unlike women who want to be mothers, who for a variety of reasons are more comfortable with the restrictions that children impose, women who are childless by choice need to feel unconfined emotionally as well as physically in order to have the autonomy and spontaneity they treasure. "I love being able to pick up and do what I want. We decide every day and every night, at the spur of the moment, without guilt or worrying about the logistics," said Myra Wyeth, a casting director whose third husband is fifteen years her junior. Dina Kahn, a bookstore owner in Richmond, Virginia, with a love of scuba diving that takes her around the world, believes the experiences that give her life meaning are predicated on her mobility. "With a child I'd be confined—I wouldn't have the privacy, the adventures, the people who are so inspiring in all the different places I've been. I would grieve if I had to give all of that up—it's a horrifying thought." Jackie Fast celebrated her love of freedom by making a film about the Beat Generation, which had inspired her. "To me it's the most important thing in the world," she told me. "If I had to live without free choice, I'd be an early suicide."

Ambition and dedication to their professions motivates many of these women to concentrate primarily on working during their childbearing years. Although other women do both, they consider it temperamentally impossible for them to devote energy to two such all-consuming projects. Actress Linda Krystal believes that in her case not being a mother was the prerequisite that permitted her to succeed in the theater. "You need an incredible amount of freedom to pursue, like a man, a career, and women who choose not to have children are trying to do that," she declared. Whenever Linda sees anyone she knows to be a "ruthless actress" extolling the newfound joys of motherhood, she confessed, "I get cynical and wonder if she just didn't get a job on Broadway."

Not to want children goes against a deeply ingrained expectation in American society. Any woman who opposes that tradition is putting herself out of the mainstream. A 1936 sociological study of voluntarily childless women ominously intoned that such behavior is "indicative of rampant individualism." Even though this choice also expresses the more subversive but equally ingrained, all-American value of the "pursuit of happiness" in one's own way, it takes a person who is willing to be different, who is comfortable (or can learn to tolerate) being a nonconformist, to question something so fundamental.

Challenging convention comes naturally to the majority of the women I interviewed. They repeatedly expressed sentiments such as "I was always different," "I like the idea that I'm different," "Even as a child I knew I was different," and "I'd rather die than conform." Having a mind of their own is an important source of their identity and self-esteem. They were the most ambitious ones; they were often the only child in their families or the only girl in town to move away, get an education, and not reproduce. Director Paula Holbrook, who chose pursuing her demanding, male-dominated career over having a family, recalls being an anomaly in Zanesville, Ohio. "In high school I was an achiever. In my town, very few women went to college; they stayed in Ohio, got married, and had children. I was the only girl that actually left the place where I grew up—everybody else still lives within a mile, including my sister.''

How did they get to be so "fiercely independent," as Jackie put it? A lifetime of thinking for themselves, often including a rebellious adolescence like Robin's, Jackie's, Simonetta's, or Tess's, prepared them to defy the status quo that prescribes motherhood and conventional roles for most women. They challenged what they considered arbitrary parental authority; they were encouraged to be daring by inspiring role models (Pam's "iconoclastic" mother, Eva's childless cousins who ran plantations); or they were prized for their individuality and determination (Nancy's mother admiringly called her "a tough little kid"). Anna Lincoln, the formerly vagabond acupuncturist, attributed her decision to the self-knowledge she had worked for years to attain. At fifty, she says, "I know myself very well. I gave myself time to find out what it is I really like—space, leisure, and time to think, to write, and to travel. This is who I am. It would be impossible to live my way with a baby.''

While a powerful streak of defiance characterizes the attitude some have toward standard notions of femininity (Linda said, "No aspect of what is traditionally associated with being a woman interests me"), the majority have no need to flaunt convention in most aspects of their lives. Jackie described herself as "such a black sheep, a rebellious teenager, sure I'd never get married," and yet, she noted, "Here I am married twenty-one years." Myra said, "I am the only one not to have a child in my family, and I'm the first divorcée, but I think of myself as a square, conventional person. Only in the context of babies am I tremendously rebellious." Their rebellion is subtle and takes the form of an independence of mind that allows them to challenge preconceived notions of how they ought to be and to accept and embrace the minority status that the choice to be childless bestows. One reason they repudiate motherhood is that a child represents someone who dictates what they should do and when, as their parents did. These women recapitulate their youthful rebelliousness by rejecting society's expectations, only this time their action is primarily self-affirming, rather than merely reactive, as an adolescent's is.

In 1987 social psychologist Sharon Houseknecht reviewed twenty-nine studies in which researchers had asked women their reasons for not having children. Their responses sounded much like what women said to me:

Freedom from child-care responsibility and greater opportunity for self-fulfillment (79%)

More satisfying marital relationships (62%)

Woman's career and finances (55%)

Disliking children (43%; probably underreported because of the stigma, since men give this response much more frequently)

Childhood experiences or fears about childbirth (33%)

However, as the stories I heard show, the deeper motives are more complicated than overt explanations suggest and have sources in the past as well as the present based upon the interplay of temperament, circumstances, and life history.

The most basic reason why motherhood does not suit a sizable minority of women is that people are not all the same. Just as thresholds of pain vary from individual to individual, so do a sense of personal boundaries, frustration tolerance, and sensitivity to constraint. There is even a broad range in how people define intrusion and autonomy and in how they react or imagine they would react to the changes motherhood brings. As Janet Frank said, "My life is not better or worse than that of a woman with children—it's just different."

The women I met have examined themselves and know that they do not have the vocation for motherhood. For them, choosing childlessness has a dual function; it simultaneously prevents them from being oppressed by certain types of duties and demands and ensures that they retain what they deem essential for their own happiness. Their personalities compel them to choose between child development and self-development. Only by refusing to do what does not fit them can they free themselves to do what matters most: to create their own independent lives.

Chapter 4

My History Created
My Solution:

Childless Women's Childhoods

IN THE YEARS I SPENT MAKING UP MY MIND ABOUT MOTHER-
hood, I realized what a crucial role my own childhood
played in the outcome and understood how much my
parents influenced who I am and how I see the world.
The women I interviewed agreed that their relationships
with their mothers were an essential ingredient in their
decisions, and many felt their fathers also had a significant impact. While the past does not determine the future, it does lay the foundation.

Every woman gets her notion of what a mother is from
her experience with her own. The mother's personality,
her relationship with her daughter, her marriage, and
how she lives her life become the basis for the daughter
of what it means to be a woman, on an unconscious as

well as a conscious level. Every daughter identifies with, rebels against, and ultimately tries to come to terms with her mother's emotional legacy.

Whatever her motives and formative experiences, any woman who chooses to be childless severs a major, literal tie with her mother and powerfully differentiates herself from her mother's life and from her own original family. Even if she loves her mother dearly, as many of my subjects do, she is not copying her in a crucial dimension—perhaps the most fundamental one from a daughter's perspective.

Whether their bonds with their daughters were terrible or terrific—and frequently they were an all-too-human combination of both—these mothers shaped their daughters' destinies and made a major contribution to their selecting a radically different way of living.

A poignant scene on Christmas Eve when she was nine years old has stuck in Melanie Taylor's mind her whole life. It epitomized her mother's devotion and explained why Melanie resolved not to follow in her footsteps: That night, Melanie's mother, a black divorcée raising two daughters alone in Allentown, Pennsylvania, picked them up at their aunt's house, where she had left them so she could work some extra hours cleaning offices. Though she had to struggle to make ends meet, it was her life's mission that her children want for nothing. Exhausted as she was, Mrs. Taylor arrived dragging the Christmas tree she had bought them. Melanie was watching when she stumbled in the doorway and skinned her knee. That slight wound came to symbolize for Melanie "the things women had to do to manage kids." "After that," she told me forty-four years later, "I said to myself I would never do this for anybody—working, worrying, scraping. I won't sacrifice myself for a child the way she did for us."

This vibrant, bohemian woman, who became a pioneering minority journalist, deduced from her mother's experience that "kids are all-consuming, and they really dominate your life." Mrs. Taylor never remarried because she worried that no man would treat her daughters properly, and so they remained her primary focus. In actuality, she was unconsciously using motherhood as a rationale for avoiding other relationships and relying on her children and her role as their mother to give her life meaning. Though she never complained, she conveyed implicitly that motherhood is martyrdom and that children were the cause of her unhappiness. Consequently, Melanie didn't want to repeat her mother's mistake by having a child who would burden her as she felt she had burdened her mother. To avoid both masochism and guilt, she rejected maternity and concentrated on her career.

But there had been another young witness to the Christmas tree incident, and she ended up having three children. It is no accident that Melanie's sister remembers the scene differently; she edited out the scraped knee and, because she identified more closely with their mother, focused instead on her mother's loving generosity. However, Melanie believes her sister, too, was affected by their mother's self-sacrificing attitude. "My sister was so relieved when her kids grew up and went out on their own; she divorced their father after that," she told me in her melodious broadcaster's voice. "Now for the first time, she's really living instead of living for everybody else. It's an awful commentary that only now can she do this—and this is somebody who loves her children."

What enabled Melanie to pick the route less common

than her sister's? Their relationship with their mother and their experiences were actually quite different. "My mother sent me to New York at seventeen to get educated and become a nurse, so I got wider exposure," Melanie explained. "I lived with an aunt who never married or had kids, and nursing school was a female environment. There were young women from all kinds of places; it was a real eye-opener." Like Eva Martinez, who spent happy summers on the plantations of her childless cousins, Melanie had inspiring mentors to show her alternatives.

Since voluntary childlessness is extremely rare among black women, I wondered whether Melanie had experienced any special pressure to reproduce. "When I was married to a West Indian man, the in-laws wanted to know when we were having kids the day after the wedding. In the black community, the rhetoric of the sixties was of nation building and of the obligation of black women to have children, but it's not as strong now from the stories I report on," she replied. Her own way of meeting what she considers her responsibility is to serve as a role model through her profession and to contribute to journalism scholarships for minority students.

Melanie's mother blamed her daughters for her own unhappiness only at a subliminal level; some mothers' accusations are far more overt. Tammy Lyons, the painter who refused to act as a surrogate for her infertile friend, bore the physical as well as the emotional brunt of her mother's distress. Tammy was the only member of the family to whom her mother confided that she had been ostracized as a child because she was half Cherokee. Throughout Tammy's childhood, this desperate woman used to fly into alcoholic rages and beat both her daughter and the husband she did not love. "My mother said repeatedly that had I not been there, she would have had the life she wanted; I prevented her. I was at fault. That made a big impression on me," she remembers. Even though Tammy came to understand that her mother's problems predated Tammy's birth, it was difficult not to blame herself. Tammy could never imagine herself in a maternal role. "As a child when we played house, I played the father, and I got up, shaved, went to work, and was out of the game, which gave me time to think while they played—that's how I became a painter," she wryly recollected. Her relationship with the nuns who taught her was her salvation; the sisters functioned both as surrogate mothers and role models. Tammy spent as much time as possible at their convent in her hometown of Tucson. With their emotional and financial aid, she moved to San Francisco in her twenties, where she studied and taught art and later married a local television personality.

Tammy worked hard to become "logical and rational—the opposite of my mother," but until recently she feared that she, too, could become abusive toward a child. Even though she now trusts her self-control, she feels satisfied with her work and her marriage without having a family. "My history created my solution," she concluded.

Despite all the pain of Tammy's relationship with her mother, they had a touching and unexpected reconciliation at her mother's deathbed. "Strangely enough, I was there when my mother was dying," Tammy told me. "I apologized to her for not having grandkids, that I'd never come through for her that way. She said she was sorry if she'd given me that impression, because she realized that my husband and I have a wonderful love relationship. 'You have each other,' she said, 'and that's all that matters.' That made me feel accepted at last."

Tammy had the opportunity to make peace with her

mother in person; choreographer Tess Clark was only able to come to terms years after her mother's death, when she herself was middle-aged. Tess's mother, who she said "only had me because in the forties women didn't refuse their husbands," rejected her and blamed her for the premature death of the father Tess worshipped, claiming that he had exhausted himself for her sake. Even as a little girl, Tess recoiled from her mother and, by extension, from motherhood. "I needed to make sure I didn't turn out like her intellectually or temperamentally, and not having children was part of that," she explained.

Open antagonism, defiance, and underlying feelings of abandonment are common in women such as Tess who make "early and absolute" choices to foreclose motherhood. Since their traumatic experiences cause them to repudiate their connection with their mothers on as many levels as possible, they have no dilemma and no wrenching decision to make.

Amy Brandon experienced neglect rather than direct hostility from a mother who was otherwise engaged. Now a forty-two-year-old reporter specializing in sensational crime stories, Amy was a "Red Diaper Baby," the daughter of a devoted member of the Communist Party. Party activities consumed all of her mother's energy, and she had very little left over for her child; she put Amy in full-time day care from the age of two—a highly unusual step in 1952. "She was a political activist as well as a serious asthmatic, and she wasn't prepared to handle kids," the earthy, candid Amy remembered. "It was a terrible time—I had the classic miserable childhood, and I don't want to replicate it." Even though she has forgiven her mother and has not completely foresworn the possibility of motherhood herself, she fears a replay of her own past from both sides. As she put it, "My greatest terror is that I would have a child that didn't like me as much as I didn't like my family and my mother didn't like me."

In retrospect, Amy can sympathize with her mother's predicament and admire her mother's commitment to her principles, if not the toll that commitment took. "She was courageous and interesting," she acknowledged. "One of her biggest struggles was that she wanted a life of her own." Extrapolating from her own youth, whenever Amy sees her ambitious, workaholic contemporaries in journalism virtually allowing nannies to raise their children, she worries that "there will be lots of furious women in the next generation." She herself is taking no chances with split allegiances, as she spends her days prowling her favorite beats, hobnobbing with detectives and street types and writing about their lives. "With my schedule," said Amy, laughing, "I can barely find quality time to spend with my dog."

Amy's present is her compensation for her past. "I don't want to come second ever again," she insists. "I'm not about to interrupt my own childhood. It's only in the last ten years that I feel I've come into my own, and I want to make up for what I didn't have. At best motherhood would be an ambivalent experience. The idea of going through more turbulence is not appealing." Afraid of needing somebody once again and risking abandonment, she only recently felt secure enough to marry the "dear, sweet, special" man she's been living with for years.

It is striking that Melanie and Amy, who were from such different backgrounds, both told me in identical words that "motherhood is all sacrifice." Each of their mothers struggled unsuccessfully with the daunting problem of meeting both a child's needs and their own.

One sacrificed herself, and the other sacrificed her child. Neither of their daughters wanted to risk a similar fate.

The degree to which the daughters in this book identify with their mothers varies widely, ranging from filmmaker Jackie Fast's "I always felt that if I did the opposite of what she said or did, I was on the right track," to sales representative Nora Adams's "I love my mother more than anything—we're kindred spirits." Quite a few extolled their mother's character, interests, and achievements outside the maternal role, but each drew the line at becoming a mother herself.

The fact that virtually every woman I interviewed attributed her decision in large part to her relationship with her mother does not mean that forgoing motherhood is primarily reactive or pathological. Women who make this choice often have a highly developed ability to think independently, solid intimate relationships, serious responsibilities, and other indications of maturity and good mental health. Other factors besides their mother, such as their father and siblings, their image of their parents' marriage, as well as circumstances and character, determined how they came to view motherhood. Nevertheless, neither choice concerning motherhood can be free of the influence of the primary mother-daughter bond.

No matter how successfully she manages to separate and how genuinely different the life she creates, a woman can still worry that she will automatically and magically be transformed into her own nemesis as soon as she gives birth. To have a child is to participate directly and concretely in another mother-child relationship, which would pull her inexorably back into her own past, evoking feelings and experiences she is relieved to put behind her. She fears either that she could turn into her mother or that a baby would feel like her mother—depriving, controlling, or intrusive.

"Don't we always fear we'll grow up to be everything we can't stand in our own mothers?" advertising executive Julie Stratton asked me, juggling two other incoming calls as we talked on the phone. Julie, who is running several simultaneous multimedia campaigns at the age of thirty-two, nevertheless dreads becoming an infantile, irresponsible, disorganized mother like her own. "I'm very scared of that responsibility, though I'm a most responsible person—I manage everything," she told me in a manner both breezy and frenetic.

Julie's awareness that her fears are unlikely to come true does not stop her from feeling them. Her entire family was "wild and crazy," including her hippie parents, who treated their children like peers and took drugs with them. "Everybody was highly dysfunctional from drugs and alcohol," she said. "Only after my brother died of an overdose did things change. It's had a huge effect; I've always been afraid I'd turn out to be the same kind of parent as my mother. She was never an adult in her life. When she was about to give birth for the first time, she said to my father, 'I can't get out of this, can I?' I grew up hearing this story. It's no wonder I'm scared."

Julie's mother was not only incompetent; she was omnipresent. "My mother was the youngest of twelve children from the mountains of West Virginia, and she clung to us like cotton on a stem," Julie related. "It was always 'fill me up, make me whole.' She didn't know how to be on her own. She didn't create her own life, and she didn't have to. Subconsciously I fear that I, too, would develop an incredible bond that would be nearly inseparable."

Much of Julie's youth was spent fleeing and rebelling. "Now it's much healthier, but our relationship used to be embattled. I was always trying to get away from her. I moved out at eighteen and in with a man, and then lived in Europe for years." At twenty-five she settled down with Jeff, an athletic, adventuresome lawyer, and found a challenging career.

Julie tries to anticipate and circumvent threats to her hard-won happiness. Recognizing that her mother's overinvolvement with her children "drove a wedge" between her parents, who divorced after the children left home, she devotes herself to making her own marriage work. "My sister has a three-and-a-half-year-old, and I've seen the effects on her relationship," Julie noted. "It's more reinforcement for my choice. Jeff has children from a previous marriage, so it was never an issue, and that was a wonderfully comfortable thing for me to step into. The effect of not having children on us has only been positive. When we're not giving time to our careers, we give time to one another—it embellishes our relationship."

As busy and satisfied as Julie is with her life, she broods about motherhood in her rare free moments. On the one hand, she relishes the "ultimate freedom" of not having anyone depend on her the way her mother did or a child would; echoing Amy Brandon's sentiments, Julie said, "for the first time in my life I'm completely enjoying myself, and I don't want to screw that up." Yet, she worries about being considered "hedonistic" by other people. She realizes that "the real pressure comes from me and my fears that I'm shirking my responsibility as a woman. It's definitely sandbags on my shoulders. I'm afraid I'll never have enough confidence and self-assurance to be a mother—I see women with babies who seem so decisive and strong, like they know exactly what to do"—a striking idealization on her part, since it's hardly true of all mothers and it's also something other women might well think about her. Julie unconsciously defines motherhood as the only legitimate criterion for competence as a woman—an issue I struggled with myself. This is an assumption she needs to address, whichever decision she makes.

Julie is still working out her feelings about motherhood and self-esteem. "The reason I've never discussed this before is that I think I'm inept and don't want to broadcast it. It's a choice that society doesn't respect. I still feel there's something definitely wrong about this decision—but I even saw a psychic who told me not to have children."

When she contrasts her own projected future with her relatives', Julie worries about having regrets later in life. "I see my mother's family, that just goes on and on," she said wistfully. "I'm afraid there'll be hell to pay, that I'll be alone and old. Society says I'll have a cold, lonely existence, with nobody around my Christmas tree, nobody to give presents to. Everybody thinks there's only one way and that's to have a baby. It's very relieving to be with people who don't."

But Julie knows she is young and is giving herself time in case she changes her mind; the prospect of having a family is not without its appeal for her. "I think we would have fantastic children—tall, athletic, and talented. And I think we would be extremely tolerant parents." Julie imagines that she would be able to transform her mother's laissez-faire attitude into something more consistently positive.

If she ultimately decides that her fears are more powerful than her longing, Julie knows she will have to deal with a loss and resolve her feelings of inadequacy. "Once I realize I definitely won't do it, we'll probably have surgery. I won't risk unwanted pregnancy; I saw too much of that. And there's no doubt that once I cross that threshold and know I can't have a child, I will grieve," she admitted. "I will be saying good-bye to an experience I chose not to participate in."

Unlike her mother, it's essential to Julie that she have her own life and her own accomplishments. "What I most want to be remembered for is for what I've done while I'm here. I'll be happy that I manage to put a smile on somebody's face. People should remember that, not a piece of me that's left."

Julie's reaction to having an irresponsible mother is to doubt her own capacity to mother. Marty Richardson, whose mother was disconnected rather than clinging, had a similar concern. "I never had a role model or got the training," the Hollywood songwriter told me. "My mother was psychologically damaged and not equipped. She approached life robotically and didn't know how to love us. I always had a curious experience of a vacuum, of somebody small and strange in charge who didn't understand who I was." Marty feels that having a child would have taken a toll on her because, she said, "I would have felt compelled to be the opposite kind of mother and to put everything into it at my own expense."

Julie, Marty, and others whose mothers had a limited capacity to nurture see childlessness as autonomy insurance. Particularly if they were eldest daughters or the only girl in the family, they felt forced to act in their mother's place and raise their siblings. For many of them, once was enough; now that they are adults with choices, they want to live for themselves. "I've been a mother already," remarked journalist Diana Russo. "I substituted for my parents, who were troubled individuals, and I was there for my sisters in ways my parents couldn't be. To me, having a child would be having to tend to someone else's life all over again."

*   *   *

No simple equation explains why women choose childlessness. A number of my subjects had traumatic early lives—but so had other women who decided, instead, to do it right the second time around, to compensate by having families of their own. And quite a few of the women I met had wise, devoted parents whom they admired and emulated in all other ways.

Even when she was a little girl daydreaming about being a torch singer in Chicago or a mountaineer in the Rockies, Barbara Cowan idolized her "quiet, remarkable" mother whose chief ambition had been to "have a carload of children." "My mother is the kind of person I want to be," she declares.

Barbara, who now represents Asian artists after living in the Orient for extended periods, chose to inhabit a very different world from her mother's, but she still speaks glowingly of her small-town Kansas upbringing fifty years ago. Her mother, a piano teacher, thoroughly enjoyed her traditional life, "loved being a mother and never complained," but Barbara observed that "she could have done more with her music." The only one of six sisters in her close-knit family not to have a large family of her own, Barbara remembers playing with dolls "in romantic roles." "My fantasies were always career-oriented; I never played mother." Barbara sees no contradiction in admiring her mother but "always want[ing] a life different from hers."

How does she explain her nonconformity? "There were a lot of us. I didn't feel deprived, but attention was equal. I tried to make myself distinctive. I was always different from my sisters. When a relative looked at photographs of me and them, he commented about that— how I had always been artistic, more interested in the creative life, and in variety." Having a career and choosing childlessness was her way to be special, to become an individual, and to compete successfully for her parents' attention.

Barbara remembers that her parents had a long and happy life together, but her comments on the effect of children on couples indicate that she subtly and subliminally contrasts her own marriage with theirs: "I don't think at all that children bring people together. Parents are always doing things simultaneously but not as partners. My husband and I really enjoy each other and our work." She's adamant about the importance of determining a woman's worth by her own achievements, independent of motherhood. "When my sister was being honored recently for her charity work, her husband went on stage and presented her with a rose for each grandchild. It really bothered me—here she was being honored for herself—that's not a proper measure of accomplishment."

She herself takes pride and pleasure in being seen as a forerunner. Though she never volunteers information about her childless status, she's happy to discuss her position if asked. "I certainly don't want to discourage anyone, but I find myself smiling and saying 'It was a choice that we made, and it was right for me.' So many younger women I meet tell me, 'I'm glad you told me that; it was important to talk to you.'"

Janet Frank, a thirty-five-year-old corporate lawyer, reached strikingly similar conclusions a generation later. "My mother was a homemaker," she told me. "She was very contented in her role, very busy, and we were extremely close. She was lots of fun to be with. I didn't want that life even though she did—I wouldn't be happy waking up each morning driving kids around. I don't think it would be good for me." Janet is fortunate to have a mother who is mature enough to appreciate that her daughter's choice is not a repudiation of her. "My mother supports me. She thinks my life is wonderful and glamorous and looks back and says, 'You have things I never could.' "

Literary agent Pam Hall's sense of autonomy was also supported by her mother, a free spirit whom she describes as "more like a friend than a parent." When Pam was twelve, her mother told her, "You're the most important thing in my life, but I have a life," and when Pam decided in her thirties to have an abortion, her mother reassured her that being a becoming a grandmother didn't matter to her, but her daughter's happiness did. Pam feels profound gratitude that she was "raised with every choice available"; her chief regret about not having children is missing the kind of rapport she and her mother enjoy.

A woman does not have to have had an untroubled childhood to appreciate her mother's good qualities. Pam's parents divorced when she was two, and Molly Barnes's stayed together even though they shouldn't have, but each woman credits her mother with nurturing her ability to think for herself. Molly, an outspoken makeup artist, told me, "I was always allowed to make up my own mind. That's the key. Nobody ever told me what I was supposed to think, and nobody ever said I was bad, stupid, or weird for not wanting to have children; I wasn't socialized that way. I was viewed with respect by my mother for making my own decisions."

The relationship between every daughter and her mother, even the healthiest and happiest, is ambivalent, fraught with conflicts between the need to move away and the need to stay connected, to emulate and to differentiate. A mother who is basically satisfied and secure tolerates these tensions, recognizes that her daughter is indeed a separate person, and encourages her to discover the varied possibilities of her own life. She wants her daughter to think for herself, welcomes but does not demand affirmation, encourages by example as well as by attitude. Choosing not to be a mother can be an expression of the freedom such a mother bestows.

Why should a woman with a genuinely happy childhood and a loving mother decide not to become a mother herself? A daughter no more mimics every aspect of a mother she adores than she necessarily discards all traces of one she detests. Wanting a child is not the only normal outcome of the identification process, and deciding otherwise does not mean that something went wrong; either choice can be valid. Whatever her limitations, a truly good mother provides the foundation for genuine choices by teaching her daughter the courage to find her own way.

Barbara and Janet believe that their mothers were perfectly pleased with traditional roles, even though they themselves wouldn't be. However, a much larger contingent of the women I spoke with detected undercurrents of dissatisfaction, such as subtle frustration or a sense of wasted talent or undue sacrifice, in their mother's lives.

Melanie's mother avoided remarriage ostensibly for her children's sake; many others stayed in unhappy marriages for the same reason. Innkeeper Nancy Sherman thinks her mother is "a great lady, very fey." But Nancy knew something was wrong when she was a child. "My mother probably felt trapped," she speculated. "She married at eighteen and had twins at twenty. My parents should have divorced, but kids precluded it." Vowing not to let the same thing happen to her, Nancy became the mate and business partner of a man who also did not want a family.

Nora Adams, the sales representative who described her mother as "a kindred spirit," was painfully aware when she was growing up that her parents had a "marriage of inconvenience." "They battled," Nora said, "but my mother assured me that having kids made it all worthwhile"—quite an unintended burden for her daughter.

A child in Nancy's or Nora's situation can easily conclude that it was she who ruined her parents' marriage or her mother's prospects, that family obligations confined her mother and forced her to sacrifice her own happiness. The daughter can conclude that her presence perpetuated her mother's distress, that she was the only reason her parents' union lasted. Whether this is true or not, she believes subliminally that they would have separated and been better off without her. Identifying both with her mother and with herself as a child, she simultaneously accuses herself of causing the pain and wants to avoid repeating it. "This could happen to me," she fears. "If I have a child, I could be stuck like my mother was." A close, childless marriage and a solid career are her protection against replicating the pattern.

Try as they may, parents cannot conceal either their personal or their professional problems from their children, and on some level children hold themselves responsible for these problems. When a mother gives up a promising career or never attempts to have one because of her family, her daughter invariably senses her unfulfilled ambition, her submerged longing for what might have been.

Casting director Myra Wyeth clearly sees her life as a reaction to her mother's dissatisfaction. As she put it, "My mother was always there; our hours were her hours. She was a teacher, but she felt obligated to make me lunch every day. She was implicitly resentful at being stuck at home, having more responsibility than she wanted to handle. It was all subliminal, but it was there. For me to select childlessness is a rejection and a criticism of how she lived." Myra understands her mother's ambivalence about her daughter's achievements. "We look alike and I do many things she wishes she would have done," she told me. "She's proud but jealous that she's not the one who got to do them."

Women differ in the way they deal with the demands of full-time motherhood. Some, like my mother and Nancy's and Myra's, throw themselves into the role and make it their career, often to the point of living vicariously through their children; Nancy described her mother as "overavailable emotionally." Others, like child psychiatrist Jane Michaels's mother, care about their families, though they have little enthusiasm for homemaking. Jane's mother would have made a terrific executive, but she was a lousy cook. In Jane's opinion, her father should have been the househusband and her mother the breadwinner. "She always had submerged bitterness about being a mother," said Jane. "She felt she had to stay home, so she missed having certain experiences." Jane is intentionally "living the life my mother would have had if she could." In her own marriage, she provides most of the income, and her husband does the cooking and housekeeping.

Likewise, Rachel Randolph, the foreign correspondent, had a mother who had worked happily as a retail buyer but who "left everything for my father and started having babies. She was furious as a young mother and never figured out why." And Paula Holbrook, who chose directing plays over having a family, had a mother who "didn't really enjoy it, although she loved me. She was bright and gave up a lot to be my mother. It made her more neurotic because she didn't have enough stimulation."

Combining motherhood with a profession was even more daunting for women of previous generations than it is today. Then there were no role models, no readily available or affordable child care, and little social support. Many of my subjects said their mothers stayed home primarily because "that was what women were supposed to do." Considering the pressures, it is understandable how few mothers succeeded in pursuing lives of their own. For example, Meredith Reynolds's mother was trained as a physicist, a rare accomplishment for a woman twenty-five years ago, but she left her laboratory to become an "excruciatingly unfulfilled" full-time housewife. Her daughter chose a demanding, bicoastal career as a publicist.

The daughters of talented, discontented women such as these don't just avoid childbearing in reaction to negative examples; they also feel inspired by their mothers. These daughters were the one in the family whom their mother chose as the repository of her own unmet aspirations. Often this encouragement is the best thing their mother gave them.

Eva Martinez, the horticulturist, witnessed her parents' unhappy marriage, but nonetheless credited her mother with encouraging her to have a profession. "My mother was trained as a lawyer and never practiced," she told me. "She was a contradiction—she didn't do what she loved, but she believed women should work and be independent. When I got a job she said, 'You'll work a little for me too.'"

Linda Krystal, the actress who decided to work in the theater full-time "like a man," went the opposite route from her mother. "My mother was an actress who gave up her career and lived through my famous and handsome father," Linda recounted. "I did it differently from her through her subtle encouragement. I felt her sadness at not fulfilling her artistic side. My mother grew to be complacently happy with the choices she made, but something was always pulling at her." Linda realized her own dreams as her mother could not and rebelled against anything remotely connected with the traditional feminine role her mother espoused. She balked at cooking and cleaning—and fortunately found a mate who didn't expect her to do either one.

Many of the women I interviewed mentioned that they were the only childless member of their families. When I asked Jane Michaels why her sister had children and she did not, she answered readily that she had accomplished what their mother aspired to and her sister had replicated what their mother actually did. Siblings do not necessarily have the same psychological parents, even though they have the same physical ones. Parents project alternative aspects of themselves onto their children and treat them differently. A child's own personality also affects her interaction with her parents. The circumstances of a mother's life can also vary dramatically when individual children are born. Hence, Melanie and her sister have different memories of the Christmas tree episode based on their different relationship to their mother.

As potent as a mother's impact is on her daughter, fathers exert a powerful influence of their own. Only a minority of the women I spoke to felt that their relationship with their fathers played a significant role in their choice to be childless, which suggests that a woman's tie with her mother is the stronger determining factor most of the time. However, for some of my subjects, the intimacy and intensity of their relationships with their fathers was a major factor in their decision. The eyes of these "Daddy's girls" still shine when they describe the man who was the central figure in their childhoods—

and some of them perpetuate the love affair for the rest of their lives.

Tess Clark, the choreographer who rejected motherhood at age eight and whose relationship with her mother had been antagonistic, was very much her "daddy's baby." She'd been his idea in the first place. "My mother never wanted kids. If she'd been a modern woman, she would have wanted to spend her life just with him," Tess told me. From the time Tess was five years old, the dimpled little redhead was her mother's rival and the star of a magical private theater her father created for her in the window of the children's clothing store he owned in Memphis, Tennessee. "He invented the concept of live models using me," Tess recalled. "He'd dress me up in different outfits, and I'd tap dance and entertain. I'd spend hours there playing with dolls, and hundreds of people would come and watch me. It was one of the attractions of downtown Memphis—people would bring their children on Saturdays. I performed for President Truman once. I was a Shirley Temple doll, so adored. My father designed this world for me; he was the center of my universe. This was where I got my concept of myself as a star."

Tess may have been her father's star, but she was her mother's bitter rival. Her mother felt jealous and excluded from this thrilling fantasy world. "She didn't want to share the man she loved with anyone," said Tess, "and when he died when I was eleven, she was grief stricken and couldn't function."

After her father's death, Tess consciously sought out childless women to imitate, since she "didn't want the life of the women around [her]." Her early decision not to have children was at once a repudiation of her mother and a resolution to have the kind of relationship with a man that she—at least in her own and her mother's mind—prevented her mother from having, as well as a way to have a man like her father all to herself. "Who made the rule that it's a sign of maturity to want to mother children and not need a man's exclusive attention?" she asked me.

Robin Green, the secretary who claimed that if she and her husband had had children, "we'd be divorced by now," was also her father's favorite. Robin's father was "a little boy who never grew up; he had the Peter Pan syndrome. My mother and I battled for his affection all the time, and I got it," Robin boasted, still triumphant over her early conquest.

Father-daughter bonds can be special and tender and wonderful, and a certain amount of competition between daughters and their mothers is universal, but any father who carries things to an extreme or who encourages blatant rivalry between his child and his wife has problems of his own. And even when both a mother and daughter believe that the daughter has alienated her father's affection, there had to have been conflicts in the parents' marriage before the child was born for such a breach to occur.

Some of my subjects consider themselves, as I did, their father's intellectual heir or even his "surrogate son." Songwriter Marty Richardson, whose mother seemed "robotic" to her, says she "got all my musical and creative ability from my father; my mother didn't understand me." Filmmaker Jackie Fast's father was an artistically talented dentist who "wished he could have been an artist and projected that onto me." And Linda Krystal was encouraged to pursue a theatrical career by a mother who gave one up, but it was her actor father who served as her drama coach for her first audition.

Even some women who admired their mothers tremendously identified more closely with their fathers.

Barbara Cowan, who admires her traditional mother, unwittingly described herself as being more like her individualistic father. "He was different from any man in our town; he stood out," she told me proudly. Like Barbara herself, "he was strong and made many unpopular decisions."

Women who are childless by choice come from every kind of background. Even though they have a slightly higher than average percentage of unhappily married or frustrated parents, their relationships with their mothers and fathers are, for the most part, indistinguishable from those of women who have children. So what makes a woman conclude that motherhood will not bring her happiness? A relationship with a mother who is masochistic, hostile, dependent, detached, or overinvolved can certainly contribute. So can a daughter's intuition that children have had a negative impact on her mother's personal or professional life, even when her mother never complains. But so profound a decision is much more than simply a reaction to what a woman sees around her, and it is not just a desire to avoid repeating her mother's negative experience. On a deeper level, a daughter frequently considers herself responsible for her mother's fate. In addition, becoming a mother would automatically force her to identify more closely than is comfortable with her own mother. A baby of her own can represent a reincarnation of the difficult mother she remembers. Motherhood would then recapitulate both sides of what a woman wants to leave behind.

A close bond with her father, her particular temperament and experience, and the presence of childless role models can broaden her horizons and make it possible for her to consider options in life that her mother may never have had. She becomes herself by being different.

Part 3

Living a Childless Life

Chapter 5

Two's Not the Loneliest Number:

Portraits of Childless Marriage

WHEN I WAS GROWING UP, I KNEW TWO CHILDLESS MARRIED women. It's striking, since one was my mother's older sister and another her good friend, that I'm not sure whether they had made conscious decisions not to have families, but in those days the subject would never have been discussed even among intimates. It's still a delicate matter to ask about. Several of the teachers who influenced me were also childless, though they belonged to a different category since they were "spinsters."

Many of the women I met, such as Tess Clark and Eva Martinez, revered childless relatives and mentors, but this was not my experience. Although I never thought about it at the time, my impressions of the two childless women and their husbands that I knew best as a child matched the popular stereotype, which, according to researchers, is as believed today as it was in the fifties: that childless women are withered and weird, unnurturant, selfish, and unsatisfied, that they dote on pets as a pitiful substitute for babies, that their lives have a hole in the middle.

My aunt Sally fit this description to perfection. I remember her chiefly for the cheerless Thanksgiving dinners I was obliged to attend at her house—the only times I saw her—at which the food was tasty (cooking was one of her hobbies) but unplentiful and I was the only child. An avid and aesthetic gardener who ran the city garden club for years, she was a sharp (she kept up with world events into her nineties, yet she'd never finished high school), stylish, and utterly self-involved woman with flaming red hair and an eternal chip on her shoulder. I saw no playfulness between her and her equally forbidding husband, my uncle Ben, an unsociable doctor who practiced homeopathic medicine thirty years before it became fashionable. The two of them seemed shut off from the world and not connected to each other either—but they lavished affection on a series of Scottie dogs, all named "Angus." Scottie memorabilia and photographs cluttered the rooms of their house, which I found alien and lifeless. The food and flowers she clearly enjoyed had no place there.

In retrospect, I'm sure my aunt was never comfortable around me and probably envied my mother her more satisfying life. Despite her talents, she was hardly a role model.

The other childless woman, my mother's friend Miriam, was more appealing. She was a prim, perfectly coiffed Canadian with a keen mind and an aura of coolness and self-containment. Even though she was actually the same age as my mother, her manner made her seem a generation older. Dinner at her house was a fastidious affair; it was the kind of place where you had to worry about making a mess or raising your voice. Miriam and her husband, Jerry, a physicist and orchid-fancier, seemed to have a genuine bond of intellect but not of sex. I remember the contrast between them and the flamboyant, fleshy flowers he cultivated.

Both of these women were accepted members of the community, with friends and interests if not professions. Still, their lives always seemed somehow different and less desirable to me than those of women with families, however tumultuous; there was something sterile, isolated, too quiet, withholding about them. Something was missing.

Most people think that all childless marriages resemble Sally's or Miriam's—and relationships like theirs may indeed have been more typical a generation or more ago, when being childless by choice was far rarer and less socially acceptable than it is currently. They are the norm no longer, but the prejudice persists. A survey of attitudes toward the childless from 1916 to the present conducted by social psychologist Sharon Houseknecht shows that they have historically been perceived as misfits who are "infantile, self-indulgent, and materialistic," and a recent Gallup Poll found that their marriages are assumed to be far less satisfying than those of people with children.

Psychologists Pollyann Jamison, Louis Franzini, and Robert Kaplan asked a large sample of subjects to rate the mental health of two couples who were described identically in every way except that one couple had chosen to have children. The "nonmother" and her spouse were perceived as less satisfied at present than the "parents" and were predicted to be less happy at the age of sixty-five. The childless couple were described as lonelier and more emotionally maladjusted, as well as less sensitive and less loving, than their counterparts with families.

Until recently, both psychology and religion have supported these assumptions. Traditional psychoanalytic theory, from Sigmund Freud through Erik Erikson, holds that parenthood is a developmental stage that is essential for emotional maturity. By implication, those who "flee" this responsibility are immature, stagnant, or stunted. Most religions concur that children give meaning and purpose to marriage, and several will not consecrate voluntarily childless unions.

The lives and loves of the childless women I interviewed challenge these stereotypes. None of my subjects—even the ones who adore their animals or who have survived rocky periods in their relationships—has a life anything like that of either of the two women I remember from childhood, and they resent the assumptions people make about them. They are candid about problems with their mates and sometimes painfully aware of their minority status in society, but they unanimously declare that they are happily married. These women believe that their exclusive, mutual bond with their husband provides something they have always wanted. Childlessness is an essential part of their satisfaction.

Contemporary voluntarily childless marriages run the gamut from couples who can hardly bear to be separated from each other to those who rarely see each other, from people who thrive on being "one person in two bodies" to those who feel that they virtually inhabit different galaxies. Some reverse or disdain traditional sex roles. According to social psychologist Sharon Houseknecht's 1979 study, the wife in a childless marriage almost always works and frequently makes more money than her husband, who tends to share household responsibilities more than most men do. Many have been married more than once, and the women are older when they first marry than most brides. There is often an unconventional dimension to these relationships. Some marry outside their ethnic or social class, and large age disparities in both directions are common, as are situations in which the couple have lived together for years but married only recently. And, contrary to what people think, these marriages tend to *last*.

Many of these same qualities are frequently found in couples with children. However, since voluntarily childless couples have chosen to focus their intimate lives solely on each other, they gravitate to relationships that facilitate the particular combination of independence and mutuality that they crave.

The prototypical marriages of Nancy Sherman, Linda Krystal, Jane Michaels, Tammy Lyons, and Joyce Rogers, as disparate as they are, have a common denominator: these women are all convinced that parenthood would make it impossible for them to sustain the bond they now have with their mates.

Pert, outgoing Nancy Sherman seems born to her role as hostess and manager of the landmark Victorian inn outside Mendocino, California, that her husband's family built in the 1880s and has lovingly maintained and restored since then. Her gracious smile and attentive manner make her guests feel they have a personal relationship with her; they might be surprised to know that the woman with the blond curls and the unassuming manner is a savvy businesswoman and researcher who published several articles on women and poverty while still a graduate student in sociology. Now forty-one, she has been married for eighteen years to Bruce, ten years her senior, the ironic, retiring heir to this spectacular estate. Theirs is a partnership on all levels.

They met as student activists at Berkeley in its radical heyday, where she was getting her Ph.D. and he was teaching American history. After graduation, Nancy got a faculty position at another college in the area. When Bruce's parents retired, he and Nancy left the university community where they had been living and working for years, moved to the country, and took over the family business with delight and trepidation.

Nancy grew up in suburban Sacramento. Her parents had little in common but stayed together for the children's sake. Her mother felt trapped and frustrated as a housewife, and her authoritarian, workaholic father held jobs as a carpenter and mechanic without much success. They fought or went their separate ways; mutuality was minimal in their marriage. So even though it wasn't easy for Nancy to leave a promising academic career to become "the boss's wife" and to sacrifice her privacy and subsume her identity into Bruce's family's, she accepted her new position because life with Bruce offered her so much that had been lacking in her parents' relationship—financial and emotional stability, social consciousness, a shared love of nature.

It was central to Nancy that Bruce, like she, desired not to have a family but instead to make their relationship with each other and the running of their beloved inn the center of their lives together.

Nancy's diminutive size, her gentle charm and soft-spoken manner, belie the directness and certainty of her convictions, which she has considered very carefully.

"Bruce told me before we married that he didn't want children, and it hit a chord immediately. We both wanted the exclusive attention, affection, and concentration of another adult. I had a twin sister, so there wasn't a chance to be the baby or the only one, and she got all the attention because she was in trouble as a child and I was the good kid. Bruce grew up at the inn, always sharing his parents with a dozen strangers." Both wanted a marriage that would compensate for their childhood deprivation.

The two of them put tremendous energy into making their marriage work. They spend their days—and a good part of their evenings—side by side in one office, running the business jointly, but with a clear division of labor; the more laconic Bruce handles the financial, behind-the-scenes end, while Nancy, the sociable extrovert, deals directly with guests. He devotes his spare time to environmental groups. Nancy's absorbing interest since her college days is her "spiritual path," which involves periodic retreats in Zen monasteries and daily meditation.

"My relationship with Bruce is very special, deep, and dear," says Nancy. "I don't want to change the equation. We wouldn't have it at this level as parents. We're playmates, we're friends, we're silly together, and we need our private time." They are both parent and child for one another, fulfilling for each other what neither had growing up.

Even though Bruce and Nancy were reasonably certain that parenthood was not for them, they wanted to make absolutely sure, and so they went for several sessions of couple counseling "to help sort it out." "We made lists of reasons why we might each want children and lists of our perceptions of each other's reasons," Nancy recounted. "That way we really got to see our own projections. I realized that one of my reasons was fear of being alone when I was old, and that's no reason to do it." The insights from their therapy gave them the final validation that they needed. "Now, even if we hit regrets twenty years from now, we know we really decided."

When they took over the business, they moved into an old frame house on the property, where Bruce and his brother had grown up. It took a while for them to get used to sleeping in his parents' bedroom, to be taking over their role and yet not be parents themselves. Even though no children share it, their home does not feel empty. Nancy and Bruce each has a study—his tan den overflows with history books and stereo equipment; her pale blue retreat, with Japanese brush paintings on the wall, is where she meditates. And even though they both feel comfortable with their choice not to have children, they still talk about it yearly, just to make sure they're in accord. They are also relieved to know that there are relatives to pass on the inn to in the future.

To Nancy's surprise and initial chagrin, her twin sister, who had also planned never to have children, had a baby several years ago. Since her sister embraced parenthood with gusto, Nancy was afraid that she would see Nancy's life as lacking something essential. Her words of reassurance meant a great deal: "I wouldn't feel sorry for you because you didn't have children—I'd feel sorry for you if you didn't have love in your life." Now Nancy is looking forward to getting to know her new nephew.

Many childless couples avoid constant interaction with families with children out of both discomfort and preference, but Nancy's position requires daily contact with people who have very different lives from hers. Even though she is comfortable with her choice, she feels the contrast between their world and her own. How does she deal with the inevitable questions from their guests about children? "They always assume we have a family, and it can be a little awkward," she said, laughing. "I joke that this place is our child substitute—we talk about it constantly, it keeps us up nights, we show pictures to everyone we meet—and we don't have to change diapers." In essence, she lets people know, defensively as well as proudly, that she not only has a "child" but has one tailored to her own needs.

A number of women told me that, like Nancy, they thought of their husbands as their symbiotic soul mates, their "best friends," even as their "twins." These couples tend to be mutually admiring and sense that they have something rare. "I'm lucky he's so terrific and we fit so well" and "we finish each other's sentences," they say. Couples like these choose to spend much of their free time together and have many interests in common.

A painful past is often one basis of their bond. Many of these women had thought of themselves as different all their lives, and when they finally found someone who suited them, they embraced the relationship with gratitude and relief. Meredith Reynolds, the publicist who has been married for fourteen years to a photographer, spoke of him with a tenderness still touched with disbelief that she had found him:

"Not having children is a representation of how we managed to come together—it's a touchstone: we are two people striving very hard not to re-create what we grew up with. I'd lived with a woman for five years after a highly promiscuous adolescence, and I came out not knowing whether I preferred men or women. He said that I thought nobody could really love me, and that he had felt the same way about himself. Now I look forward to coming home and seeing him and feel sad on Monday morning when I say good-bye to him. We are very much in love, and I wake up every day saying 'I can't believe this.' "

*   *   *

Another type of marriage popular with voluntarily childless women is the complementary, opposites-attract variety, in which the couple is stimulated by the differences between them. Often in these dual-career couples, the woman also behaves in ways that are not typically considered "feminine."

When a woman decides not to have a family in order to devote much of her energy to her career, she needs a partner who will support her efforts and adjust his lifestyle accordingly, someone who doesn't need dinner on the table—or even expect her to be *at* the table—many nights of the week.

Linda Krystal, the statuesque blond actress, found this situation with Kevin when she was thirty-five. Her main priority until then had been studying and establishing her career in the theater, which had won her Emmy nominations for her Ibsen and Chekhov interpretations. Her drama coach for her first audition monologue, which landed her a coveted role in a Tennessee Williams play for her debut, was her father, a dashing and successful actor. Though she greatly admired him and was devoted to her mother, a marriage like theirs was the last thing she wanted. She worked hard not to follow in her mother's footsteps. "My mother had several cancers throughout my life, and I associated submerging myself like she did with not being healthy," she explained. The traditional feminine role became anathema to Linda.

Linda had been in love with several of her leading men earlier in her life, but none of the relationships lasted. No one filled the bill until she met Kevin. She knew that the sturdy, bright-eyed occupant of the adjoining seat on the red-eye from Los Angeles, where she'd been filming her first TV pilot, was the man for her from his opening conversational gambit: "I'm a journalist covering a transvestite convention for *Esquire*. Do you have any idea how hard it is to find pumps in men's size twelve?" Here was her complement.

Kevin, they quickly established, didn't require a conventional wife; he'd been miserably married to one at an early age and had two grown children. This forty-year-old writer specializing in the offbeat offered Linda the necessary combination of support and freedom, tempered with humor. And she was convinced children would have wrecked it all:

"He said when we talked about it that having a child would end us because of my aversion to housekeeping and his unwillingness to participate. I knew that with him the woman would have had to take care of everything."

Linda is true to her word. She is a most attentive hostess, and dinner parties at the Krystals' house are lively affairs, but the food is always Chinese takeout. She and Kevin spend months at a time on opposite coasts, with huge long-distance bills and occasional weekend reunions. When her father was alone and dying last year, she moved to Florida for six months to take care of him. Even when she and Kevin find themselves together in their informal, book- and dog-filled Los Angeles home for any length of time, they have opposite schedules to suit their different temperaments: he writes from midnight to eight A.M. every night and socializes when he's not working, she's an early riser and a homebody.

Despite their many dissimilarities, Linda and Kevin share what for them are the fundamentals. They became Quakers (his parents were lapsed Catholics, hers nominal Episcopalians), and the theater is central for both of them. Every role she creates or novel he writes, the other critiques. In recent years, to counteract the dearth of substantive parts for mature women, he's been writing screenplays for her.

With all Kevin's charm, wit, and devotion, he is not an easy man for Linda to live with. His struggles with writer's block have been Promethean. His compulsion to hand print every word (a word processor would cheapen his craft) has caused a nagging case of carpal tunnel syndrome, and his undeserved bouts of self-doubt can last late into the morning. There have been periods when she had no work and he got bad reviews, when they've been lonely apart and grated on each other when they were together. He is as brazen and tactless as she is demure and reticent. Their basic bond has weathered it all.

Other voluntarily childless couples actually reverse roles, the woman earning the bulk of the income and the man keeping house. Such unusual arrangements are much more common among the childless than anybody else, since these couples tend to be less identified with traditional sex roles, more comfortable defining their own division of labor.

Max and Jane Michaels have exchanged roles as their relationship has evolved over the past thirteen years. Hip, clever Max intrigued and attracted Jane when they first met folk dancing in Central Park in the summer of 1980. "The only thing we have to decide now," he whispered after their first dance, "is what we're having for breakfast." She was a modern dancer supporting herself by teaching aerobics at a health club, and he was a freelance commercial artist whose work had originality and flair but limited commercial success because he distained "establishment" clients. Financial problems compounded with Max's fear of commitment (it took him a year to introduce Jane to his friends) made the auburn-haired six-foot-tall thirty-year-old despair of any permanence with him; "I'd have to win the lottery for this to work," she complained—and then she did. It was only twenty-five thousand dollars, but it was enough to get them started. The cynical, fortyish confirmed bachelor proposed at a fifties-rock revival concert to the strains of "Earth Angel."

Jane was tiring of the life of a struggling artist. The windfall dramatically changed their prospects and galvanized Jane's, if not Max's, aspirations. She decided to go to medical school, as she had always wanted to do. This meant more years of straitened circumstances, but Max gave her his wholehearted support. He wasn't threatened by having a wife with an M.D. when he hadn't gone to college and was quite content to be her part-time househusband (she's messy, he's a neatnik), doing the cooking, crafting built-in furniture. However, two conditions had to be fulfilled: they keep their separate apartments on opposite sides of town (he held on to this symbol of independence for the first five years) and have no children. That sort of responsibility was unthinkable to him; he had enough trouble making a commitment to another adult.

Marriage on his terms agreed with Max. He came to rely on Jane in ways he never thought possible, and he mellowed considerably. He stopped smoking, cut down on his drinking, took up kung fu, and became, to the astonishment of his friends, both faithful and a snuggler.

Max was nonnegotiably opposed to parenthood, but Jane, like a number of women I spoke to, could have gone either way—and might have become a mother if she'd had a willing mate. Jane sees that Max's foreclosure of parenthood released her from the responsibility of struggling with her own conflict in a more active way and understands that marrying him was her way of deciding de facto. Working as a pediatric psychiatrist compensates for any loss she may feel; her child patients provide her enough intimate, ongoing contact with children to satisfy her.

Women who choose to be childless often construct a life in contrast to their mother's. Like Linda, Jane believes she has the marriage and the life her mother secretly craved and which would have satisfied her. "My mother was a talented, ambitious administrator—she should have been the one working full-time rather than my father. I think I made the choice she didn't make; I'm living the life she would have lived if she could." By not having a child herself, she hopes to avoid her mother's frustration.

The role reversals of their marriage are not entirely comfortable for either Jane or Max; sometimes he feels inadequate and depressed even though he refers to her proudly as "my wife the doctor." She doesn't mind having the higher income but does want him to be more satisfied with his work and is delighted that her practice is finally bringing in enough money that they can start looking for a more commodious place to live with a studio for him.

He and his wife have traded roles financially, but the rugged-faced Max is thoroughly masculine in every other arena. The only time he's not dressed in a work shirt and jeans (he likes to brag that he last wore a suit thirty-seven years ago at his bar mitzvah) is when he dons his blue uniform and bullet-proof vest on his weekly beat as a volunteer policeman. Jane has taken charge of her career, but like many a woman in a more conventional marriage, has had to learn to stand up for herself in the face of Max's tendency to want his own way in what they do and where they go together. She's happy to finally be in the position to veto the rock-bottom accommodations he favors and insist on a modicum of comfort when they travel. And now that the rigors of her medical training are over, she's struggling to find the time to start dancing again.

Though Jane's husband insisted on no children as a condition of their marriage, for some childless couples, children were "supposed" to have been essential. Friends and family worked overtime to convince Les and Tammy Lyons that having children together was practically their karma, and yet their marriage has flourished without them.

It started with their meeting. "Here is the man who'll be the father of your kids," said the knowing friend who introduced them—which caused Tammy to avoid Les the whole evening until he cornered her, and she discovered to her consternation that her friend might be right.

Tammy, who had virtually been adopted by nuns in Tucson and had declined to have her friend Joan's baby for her, inauspiciously met Les shortly after that painful incident. He was the thirty-seven-year-old host of a popular local television talk show in San Francisco.

Les turned out to be the only man the stocky, boyish twenty-five-year-old had ever known whom she felt she could depend on. And not only was he not threatened by her work or jealous of her devotion to it, but he "fell in love with it"; he had had dreams of becoming a painter himself and recognized her superior talent. He made her feel sexy, and he was even willing to do dishes. This combination melted Tammy's remaining reservations about matrimony, although she still had major doubts about motherhood.

To their consternation, the baby "campaign" that had preceded their meeting escalated when they decided to marry. Unbidden, Tammy's gynecologist informed her that pregnancy would be good for her hormone imbalance. Since Les's brother was a bachelor and his sister had had herself sterilized years before, his family made sure he was reminded that he was the only source of potential grandchildren. Les's mother called the day after the wedding to make Tammy promise not to raise the child his mother naturally assumed they would produce as a Catholic. When, after long deliberation with Les, Tammy decided not to try to conceive for the foreseeable future, another friend approached her at a party and said, "How can you waste his genes?"—evidently not thinking hers worthy of consideration. "Her remark made me feel there was no solidarity among women," Tammy reported, still incredulous at her friend's presumption.

The pressure Tammy felt to have a baby with Les was not entirely external, even though she knew she would never have even considered it with anybody else. "My doubts are only in relation to him. He wouldn't want to adopt, so I'd have to do it. He's much more relaxed and confident than I am." Was she depriving the man she adored of something he would have enjoyed and been good at? Was she being selfish (the worst sin she could have imagined as a girl) because she wanted him to herself? "I already have to share him with his TV audience and his family," she explained. "It's difficult to think of also sharing him with a twenty-year guest." For his part, having a child would have been fine with Les if Tammy were comfortable with it, but he accepted her self-doubts and let her make up her own mind.

Tammy worries about wanting anyone's exclusive attention or disappointing other people's expectations and has a tendency to feel uncomfortable about putting her own needs first. So they haven't entirely shut the door on the possibility of children even after ten years of marriage, and sometimes "play devil's advocate" for each other. They weigh the pros and cons, and end up deciding to maintain the status quo.

Meanwhile, they love the life they've made together. They each have work that engrosses them and intrigues the other. Tammy's studio is in their Chinatown apartment, and Les knows every chef in the neighborhood. Tammy's work decorates several of the tonier local restaurants. A couple of years ago a stray firecracker on Chinese New Year started a fire in their place that destroyed all her paintings and damaged most of their books and clothes. They stayed with friends for six months, living out of suitcases, and grew even closer as a result. But no long-term intimate relationship is immune from problems, and one of theirs is that the voluble, opinionated Les likes to be the center of attention, and Tammy, who has always expressed herself more easily through painting than in words, has to fight to be heard.

Any amount of guilt Tammy might have had for not doing her "'duty" was assuaged recently at her mother's deathbed, when her mother was able to reassure Tammy that her marriage with Les was the most important thing, even if it hadn't produced offspring.

The pressure to reproduce that Les and Tammy faced wasn't so hard for them to resist because it was mostly external; when the pressure comes from within the relationship, things can get truly difficult. What does a couple do when the woman has decisively ruled out children and the man changes his mind?

This is the predicament that unexpectedly confronted Joyce Rogers ten years into her marriage with Robert, her second husband. She'd originally married her college sweetheart right after graduation, and the two of them spent their first year traveling around the country doing odd jobs. When they settled down in Boston, she told me, "he started lobbying for children." Joyce, a lean, frank, no-frills brunette, was one of those women who was distant from her own parents, did not remember ever feeling feminine, and, as a consequence, had "always" been quite clear that motherhood did not suit her. She never experienced the kind of desire she thought she would need in order to undertake it. Since she believed she couldn't help but be the dutiful, resentful parent her own mother had been, she and her husband divorced, and he eventually had a family with his second wife. Joyce went to work as a copy editor on a political magazine and began writing fiction. She found the solitary literary life to her liking.

Fifteen years later, after a variety of short-lived affairs, this austere and somewhat reclusive woman fell seriously in love with her next-door neighbor Bob, an insurance executive who was estranged from a wife he found hysterical and immature. Joyce's self-containment and independence appealed to him, and his exuberance attracted her. She liked the fact that he was a successful businessman who loved vintage jazz, played a mean trumpet, and appreciated literature. Bob found in Joyce the equal partner and companion he realized he needed, a refreshing change from a woman who seemed to insatiably demand his attention. Joyce appreciated the way Bob pushed her to get an agent for her novels and encouraged her to have more fun. She enjoyed his friends, his tastes, and the way he respected her need for time alone to read and write. He divorced his wife and married Joyce within the year.

Forty by now, and beginning an early menopause, Joyce made it clear to Bob that children were "out of the question." Even though Bob would have liked a family, he decided that finally finding the right woman to share his life meant more to him. He respected Joyce's honesty and accepted the validity of her feelings, and he knew motherhood wouldn't make her happy. It all seemed very abstract, logical, and mutual at the time. They lived contentedly together for the next ten years, she now writing fiction full-time at home, while he supported her.

Then Bob's father died. They had been estranged for years and had reconciled only in the months leading up to his death from heart disease. The grieving Bob suddenly found himself longing for a child—preferably a son. He had rebuilt the family tie to the past and now needed to extend it into the future. A desire he had given up almost effortlessly a decade earlier now felt like an urgent necessity for him. He begged Joyce, who was almost fifty, to consider adopting.

Although Joyce sympathized with Bob, she knew that becoming a mother was an emotional impossibility for her. "He badly wanted a baby, but he works from six A.M. to ten at night," she said. "I told him I'd be like a single parent—did he expect me to run around after a four-year-old? I said, 'If you feel that strongly, we should end this right now' "—though she hoped he wouldn't. They had nights of tears, raised voices, and strained silences, as they struggled to decide what to do.

They didn't end it, but it took six months of marriage counseling and many fights and sleepless nights, to work it out. They both expressed feelings of resentment, depression, anger, and fear—and decided that they loved each other too much to separate. "The fact that I'd been clear from the beginning helped me get over my concern that I was depriving Bob, and his letting me know that he knew who he was getting when he chose me helped too," Joyce told me. Though their mutual feelings of disappointment have not vanished, the intensity has diminished. Two years later, she said, "Bob still

137

has twinges when we spend a weekend with friends and their toddlers, but he's compensated by getting close to his sister's little boy." Although the parenthood conflict didn't end up destroying Bob and Joyce, it sorely taxed them.

All of these couples, as different as they are from one another, agree that not having children is an integral part of their relationship. Whether the decision was mutual like Nancy and Bruce's, overtly unilateral like Jane and Max's, inevitable like Linda and Kevin's, or problematic like Tammy and Les's, they all feel that their bond is special and could not have been maintained if they had had a family. They know that the dynamics of a couple *must* change when a child enters the picture, and it is the dynamics they currently have that they treasure.

At first glance, Bob and Joyce's marriage seems an exception to this rule, since they were deeply threatened by his desire for a child. However, had they been less committed to each other or their foundation been less solid, they could never have withstood the tension. Bob's change of heart could well have spelled the end for their marriage, as so often happens when couples disagree on something as fundamental as parenthood. What ultimately enabled them to resolve their conflict was precisely his conviction that she was the most important thing in his life.

The lives that these couples have created for themselves are worlds away from the truncated lives of my aunt Sally or my mother's friend Miriam and reflect a reality quite different from the sorry popular stereotype but very much in keeping with research findings about marriage without children today. Like the women I interviewed, the large sample of childless couples studied by psychologists Linda Silka and Sara Kiesler were just as content with their lives as couples who were parents; the only striking difference was that their relationships were more egalitarian. Other studies report high levels of harmony, closeness, and an unusual level of direct communication in childless couples; since nobody else is competing for their attention, they say, they have a harder time avoiding dealing with each other even if they want to.

Scientists used to assume that childless marriages were unhappier because some studies reported a higher divorce rate, but they have now come to believe that unhappy couples may simply find it easier to separate when they can't rationalize staying together "for the sake of the children." Sharon Houseknecht's recent study of fifty carefully matched couples finds that childless marriages are typically good, close, and long—"cohesive and satisfying." These couples' degree of happiness, sexual fulfillment, determination to stay together, mutual interests, and level of agreement were consistently higher than they were among couples with children—and the childless husbands did more of the housework.

The marriages I saw had staying power; the average length was ten years. There was a striking sense of closeness, camaraderie, and the ability to work together and apart in these couples. Their energy goes into their careers, their interests, and each other. They feel no gap in their lives; as sales representative Nora Adams said, "I feel very happy and comfortable with just my husband and our two dogs. Our home is complete; I don't think anything is missing." And visiting the Shermans, the Lyonses, or the Krystals is a radically different experience than Thanksgiving at my aunt's house.

Even though they have basically what they want, several women I spoke to did express the same sorts of regrets about not having children with their husbands as Tammy Lyons did. "He's so fun-loving and exuberant, he'd make a great dad," said playwright Simonetta Fracci. She believes that children are the one natural expression and continuity of mutual love that she was sorry would be missing from her otherwise terrific relationship with Jake. Like Bob Rogers, Cindy Gardner's husband, Randy, recently realized how much he wants to be a father, at the same time as it became evident to her that she really didn't want to be a mother. "It feels terrible to disappoint him," she confessed, "but this is the one issue in marriage where compromise simply isn't possible."

Women repeatedly cited the special quality of their marriages as one major factor in their not wanting to have children and expressed fear of interfering with their one-to-one intimacy. "It's too good to risk changing the chemistry," they told me. "Childlessness embellishes our relationship." A child would be an interloper, as they themselves may have felt (consciously or unconsciously) they were between their own parents. Pam Hall, who found happiness with her second, non-daddy-material husband, explained her point of view. "If you take the children away, you have to have something more vital together; not having them actually enhances things between us. I notice that when his children are around all sexual spontaneity goes—it's no wonder people with children have a hard time enjoying sex. Our conversation and our intimacy are about us, not diverted to, by, and for anybody else." The lack of private space and time for both sex and conversation, which many parents lament but learn to manage, looms especially large for a part-time stepmother like Pam, and she prefers the lack of constraint that she usually enjoys.

Myra Wyeth, the fifty-year-old casting director, met her third husband in an acting class. He is an artist fifteen years her junior, and they live mostly on her salary. She describes their ten-year-long marriage as "very romantic, centered on just the two of us." She values his optimism, his aesthetic sense, and, most of all, the way he cares for her: "Because there are no children, we can fully give ourselves to each other, and I want that; with little kids, for a long time the primary attention goes to them. I wanted to share my life with a man and for us to be the primary focus, and I see that as a substantial difference in expectations out of life."

The consensus among these couples is that their commitment to each other is facilitated by childlessness. They are realistic about the fact that having children, as meaningful and gratifying as that can be, changes a marriage and must interfere significantly with the kind of intimacy, freedom, and focus two adults can share alone. They can't be both Nick and Nora Charles *and* the Cosby family. They know they can't have everything.

There are factors in the childhoods and personalities of many childless women that make a "just the two of us" relationship seem appealing. While some, such as Nancy Sherman and Meredith Reynolds, never got as much attention as they needed as children, quite a few women I interviewed had been their father's favorite and their mother's overt or covert rival when they were growing up. Marriage without children is a way for these women to reproduce something precious from the past, to attain completely what their mothers never had, because of them, and they had only partially, because of their mothers: a man's exclusive love.

Voluntarily childless marriage is a combination of

compensation, recreation, and celebration. In their husbands, some childless women discover their fathers again. Others construct the kind of mutual admiration, attention, and support that they craved and could not have consistently as children. They feel they have really found a marriage of true minds, without impediments.

Chapter 6

No Gene
for Motherhood:

Forging an Alternative
Feminine Identity

ONCE A WOMAN FACES HER PERSONALITY AND HER PAST AND
makes the decision not to have a child, she confronts
another equally daunting task: on what is she going to
base her identity as a woman and as a person now that
she has renounced the traditional defining role? What is
her relation to a society of parents and families? What
will give her life meaning? Motherhood automatically
brings status, structure, and a sense of purpose. Anybody who accepts what Jean Veevers, the first researcher
to study voluntary childlessness, called "the parenthood
prescription" (i.e., having children), thereby "joins the
ranks of the mature, the secure, the respectable, and the
adult." None of this comes easily to a nonmother; she will
always be fundamentally different from most other

women she knows. She must design her destiny for herself and deal with the world's reaction to her nonconformity.

Motherhood confers a built-in identity. Very few men, but countless women, can reply "I'm a parent" when somebody asks them what they do. Many of these full-time mothers love their job, and it suits and satisfies them. Some, though, stay home by default or out of anxiety, retreating into the family circle, away from competition or external expectations. In either case, a mother can derive her self-esteem primarily from her domestic duties, immersing herself in that preordained, culturally sanctioned, compelling occupation for most of the rest of her life. Childless women don't have that option.

The focus of a mother's activity and a major source of her identity is her relationship with her child; her day and her time are structured externally for her by her child's needs. No equivalent niche exists for a woman without a family. Unless she unwisely attempts to live through her husband, she must provide her own, internal structure. Her self is her only center; independent action alone defines her. Like a man, she cannot simply be; she must do.

Motherhood is not, of course, the sole raison d'être for every woman who has a child. Many consider their careers, their other intimate relationships, and activities unrelated to their children to be just as essential. But, unlike a childless woman, a mother doesn't *have* to do anything else to earn a legitimate place in this or any other society; she has a traditional role to fall back on, a "natural" place in the order of things.

Many of the mothers I know who have full-time careers applauded the women in this book and had no trouble empathizing with their point of view, even though they themselves had made a different choice.

Several even confided that they weren't sure they would have had families if they had known what it entailed. However, many of the childless women I spoke to encountered disturbing undercurrents of negative sentiment and unexpected prejudice against them. Strangers impugned their femininity, implying that they were cold and unfeeling, and their own families questioned their morality and maturity.

Filmmaker Jackie Fast got a firsthand glimpse of the underside of public reaction to childlessness once on the red-eye from Los Angeles. Although she'd never felt any overt prejudice personally before, the experience so shocked her that she considered it "my metaphor for how many people really feel about us": "Across the aisle from me was a crying baby and its parents. In front of them was a woman around forty-nine, who looked like a magazine editor, well turned out. Five times, very politely, she asked the child to stop kicking her seat. The sixth time she raised her voice a little, still more controlled than I would have been—and the parents screamed at her, 'You're just jealous that you don't have kids.' I got livid and called a flight attendant. Then the plane broke up into factions. Some people backed us up, but a bunch started yelling at her things like 'You're past your childbearing years, you dried-up old hag,' and at me that I was a malcontent. This was very shocking to me; I was her."

What's particularly revealing about Jackie's tale is that her fellow passengers had no way of knowing that she and her alter ego were childless; they simply assumed that only a childless woman would react negatively to this kind of behavior.

Sales representative Nora Adams also had a remarkable public encounter concerning her childlessness. She was having lunch with an old friend in Chicago. "I was telling her how comfortable I was about my choice not to have children," Nora recounted. "A total stranger came over and said, 'I really would rethink that decision; you'll be sorry.' My jaw dropped. She knew nothing about me—I could have been an ax murderer—and yet she felt qualified to tell me to reconsider the most personal decision of my life." The stranger's belief about how all women ought to behave was so challenged by what she overheard that she felt both entitled and compelled to intervene.

Expressing unpopular sentiments like Nora's makes some people uncomfortable. After my article on my own decision was published, I received an anonymous letter from "a concerned colleague" urging me to reconsider. Although we had never met, my correspondent insisted that I was deluded to imagine that such a course of action could come from self-knowledge. The "real" explanation was avoidance caused by fear, which (she was sure) I would regret for the rest of my life. According to her analysis, my action demonstrated that I had failed to resolve my relationship with my mother successfully. She even suggested that I should go back into therapy in order to change my mind. Like Jackie and Nora, I concluded that what I did, particularly since I put it in writing, must have threatened the status quo. People can become anxious and intolerant when someone challenges their worldview, especially about so hallowed an icon as motherhood. As Pam Hall put it, "Childlessness is un-American; it's like being a traitor to your flag."

Being treated like an outsider causes resentment in childless women because it reinforces their minority status. "People in the majority don't realize they're prejudiced," says lyricist Marty Richardson. "It astonishes me that they ask if I want kids and then look at me oddly when I say I don't. I wish I felt comfortable turning the tables and asking them why they want them."

Nina Andrews, a twenty-three-year-old law student, is dismayed that some educated women of her generation continue to stigmatize childlessness. "My friends sit around and talk about when they'll get married and have kids, like it's an automatic thing. They can't believe that I don't want to have children. It makes me angry that they're disregarding and rejecting. I thought women were supposed to support choice." Nina hopes to devote herself to gender issues in her law practice, a specialty that both cements her own feminine identity and has an impact on the world. "I see law as the best way I can help change the status of women," she says.

Casting director Myra Wyeth is convinced that covert antichildless sentiment once cost her a job. "A producer asked me during an interview if I planned to have a child. I answered, 'I'm too into my work and my husband. You can't be superwoman and do everything. I've selected the things I want to give primacy.' In the back of his eyes there was a little tiny look, and I could see he was thinking, 'Maybe she's a ballbuster.' He hired somebody else." Myra believed that the fact that she was so clear about her priorities, as well as what those priorities were, intimidated her potential boss because she seemed unfeminine to him.

The insensitivity of family and friends hurts even more. Although some women did report that their families proudly backed their unusual choice, a surprising number were stung by the tactlessness and even the hostility they encountered. Barbara Cowan's sister's covert competition with her surfaced in a "helpful" suggestion that Barbara write about her cat in the family newsletter, since she had no children whose achievements she could report.

The pressure that some families feel justified in exerting can be remarkably blunt. Jennifer Samuels, a twenty-four-year-old who was just beginning graduate study in social work and had no boyfriend, was informed by her parents at a relative's funeral that they expected her to name their prospective grandchild after the deceased. These presumptuous remarks were prompted by their conscious fear that they would have no heirs, as well as an unconscious worry that their daughter's decision reflected badly on them.

The desire for grandchildren can make conservatives out of the most untraditional families. Advertising executive Julie Stratton's hippie parents, who took drugs with their children in the seventies, treat their errant daughter like a delinquent. "In my family it's the expected thing," Julie reported. "They're from West Virginia, where that's the only way. Nobody's ever said anything direct, but they look at me and talk funny to me. They want to know why. I tell them I'm not interested, and they react in disbelief, like I'm joking. How could I possibly not have that desire? My mother makes faces and says, 'Do whatever you want, but I hope you change your mind.' " Her parents' disapproval makes Julie feel guilty and increases the sense of personal defectiveness she is battling as she makes her final decision.

Shortly after Myra's third marriage at the age of forty, her parents and in-laws sat the newlyweds down in their breakfast nook for a serious talking-to. "They all seemed desperate to be grandparents," Myra recalled. "His parents said, 'You're getting old. You can go off and we'll raise the child.' And my mother concurred. I laughed, but my husband was aghast. My father got furious and said, 'You have no sense of responsibility.' I replied, 'My sense of responsibility is highly developed—I can't take care of them. The world is full of unwanted children—if you want one, go get one.'"

Myra was annoyed but unfazed by her experiences with the producer and with her family because she feels so comfortable with her decision. "Though you're regarded as somewhat unfeminine if you're not that type of nurturer, it gives you freedom, and with that freedom comes the potential for a kind of power that many women do not feel they have," this compact, curvaceous woman told me. She frankly compared her life with that of a woman with children. "A mother's image of herself in the world isn't the same as mine; perhaps hers is larger. She sees herself in the continuity of generations, as I do not—but the world can go on without my genetics." Myra understands her limits, recognizing that she has a marriage that suits her, a job that stimulates her, a solid sense of herself—and plans to go back to work as an actress in her old age. She believes that "to do something you really want makes you feel like more, not less."

Stockbroker Mimi Davis feels the same way. "Lots of people have children by rote, because it's the thing to do; they don't think. In my opinion, they should be envious of a woman who decides not to because she's done what she wanted, not what's expected or what everybody does."

Mimi had to deal with doubts about her femininity before she reached this conclusion because, like many women, she feared that being different from the norm was pathological. Her lack of ambivalence made her feel particularly odd. "I never had a maternal instinct, a sense that that's why you got married. It worried me that I didn't have the same feelings as everyone else, but I thought it would come." Medical problems exacerbated her psychological concerns and forced her to make an early decision. "Since I have cystic ovaries, my body doesn't behave like a woman's is supposed to, so doctors pressured me at thirty to have a child right away. 'Doesn't it matter if my husband and I want one?' I asked them." The urge that Mimi awaited never came, and she prides herself on her refusal to yield to the pressure of either time or external authority. "I did the right thing then, and I feel very vital now," she declares.

Considering some of the reactions childless women evoke, it is not surprising that many of them worry about whether they are normal. Novelist Joyce Rogers's gynecologist actually sent her for a psychiatric consultation in 1963 after she expressed her intention to him. "He said it was neurotic to feel that way, so I went— something I would never do today," Joyce recounted. "The psychiatrist was a strict Freudian and hardly said a word. He didn't change my mind."

What does change is the way a woman interprets other people's opinions once she resolves her internal conflicts about motherhood, as bookstore owner Dina Kahn discovered: "I got lots of comments from colleagues and other women with children; they'd say 'why don't you— don't you like—you ought to—you need to—you really should—you'd be a happier person.' They used to throw me off balance, and I spent years trying to deal with it. I'd feel comfortable with my decision until challenged or criticized, and then I'd think that something was wrong with me. Finally I smartened up and started analyzing what was going on with *them.* The underlying message was 'What's wrong with you? You're not reinforcing my choice.' Some of them I was making uncomfortable. Some of them disapproved of or envied me. I was very proud of myself and what I'd done—I'm a scuba diver, and I've traveled all over the world. I was exuberant and happy, and some of them weren't so happy with their lives. All of this makes people uncomfortable, and they don't tolerate somebody out of the ordinary." Dina's reaction to the motherhood lobby is partially compensatory, but her analysis of their motivation is accurate, nonetheless; each side raises questions for the other.

Long after they have come to terms and are living comfortably with their decisions, many nonparents feel a sense of being subtly excluded from the world of families that surrounds them. "I'm not part of the community in New Jersey where I live," journalist Diana Russo said. "There it's the mommy club when you have a child—suddenly you're everybody's sister. My own sister has four children, and I feel left out; I'm just the aunt." Marty Richardson found Los Angeles surprisingly family oriented when she moved there from the East Coast. "If you opt out of parenthood, it's hard to find connections," she said. "It's been tough to carve my own niche here."

Women from all parts of the country expressed similar sentiments, but Southerners complained the most. When Susan Bartlett moved to rural North Carolina after she retired from her Ivy League psychology professorship, she was struck by the prevalence of intergenerational families in her new home and by the centrality of children in the lives of her contemporaries. "Living in the South, where kinship is so important a value, it's incredible how much time women in my age bracket spend taking care of grandchildren," she said. "Here the first two questions are 'What church do you go to?' and 'Do you have children?'" It took her several years to adjust to being the only woman among her acquaintances without church or family ties. Maintaining relationships with several of her former students, whom she calls her "surrogate daughters," helps. Dina Kahn noticed a difference in people's sense of personal boundaries when she moved from Indianapolis to Richmond, Virginia, to open her bookstore. "Down here," she said, "the intrusiveness level is a little higher. People ask about your personal life more than in the Midwest—I was shocked at the questions I'd get. In the Midwest people are more reserved and conscious of privacy."

New York City got the highest marks for tolerance of individualism. Fund-raiser and adoptive Manhattanite Hope Walker believes that "New York City is one of the greatest places in the world to be without a child. People are far more accepting here than in Canton, Michigan, where all the women on the block thought I had moved in to steal their husbands. New Yorkers allow things to coexist. You can get away with anything here, and you're not judged as inadequate because you're not a mother."

Childless women adapt to life in such seemingly unlikely places as small towns, rural areas, and suburbs, but they have to make an effort to find a place for themselves, since they often constitute a minority of one. While they may appreciate other aspects of life in these locales, they need an unusual degree of self-confidence and self-acceptance of being different to make it work.

The best antidote for the feeling of disconnection is a network of like-minded friends. Most of my subjects, wherever they live, have created a peer group for themselves that feels indispensable. "I have relationships with people who admire me for the strength of my convictions," Tess Clark told me. "They've guided and supported me." Jackie Fast believes that her friends, most of whom are childless, insulate her and allow her to live in an environment that suits her, where family life is less important than friendship.

Unconscious jealousy and the compulsion to proselytize for parenthood are not universal among people with children; many members of the majority admire and encourage others who make the less popular choice. When fashion stylist Christy Nichols worried that her intention not to have children meant she was abnormal, her therapist's reaction was quite different from Joyce Rogers's; he asked her, "By whose standards are you judging?" and encouraged her to think for herself. To her delight, Christy later found that her decision had an unexpected perk: "I thought the men I dated would be horrified, but instead they were relieved and relaxed that I wouldn't run after them to have babies. One said I was a single man's dream date—beautiful, don't have kids, don't want kids, and her mother's three thousand miles away; what more could he want?"

A woman who has made a well-considered decision to become a mother, who acknowledges her own ambivalence, can look with appreciation and empathy on the life of someone else who chooses otherwise. One unusually self-aware acquaintance of mine, who gave up a flourishing legal career when her third child was born, wrote me this note when she read the same article as my "concerned colleague":

> ... I think of you often—your travels to exotic countries, your professional pursuits: in short, your adult life. Suburban motherhood is wonderful in many respects; there are moments so golden that they take my breath away. This is, however, also an extremely circumscribed existence. Not surprisingly, part of me craves your life. It helps to know you are out there, visiting unusual places, sampling wonderful new food, meeting intriguing people. So I'll remember you when I'm hiding with the older boys and preparing to ambush the latest bad guy or rocking the baby in the darkness.

She understood, as I had, that there are no lives without limitations, no choices without losses.

Most of the women I interviewed, especially those who had reached middle age, had attained a sense of peace and pride about the path they had chosen. They had come to recognize, as Robin Green expressed it, that "there's no gene for motherhood"—no universal maternal instinct the absence of which marks them forever as deficient in womanliness. Nevertheless, like everyone who elects to live outside the norm, each of them had to find her own way to cope with the palpable proof that she was different from the majority in that critical dimension.

These nonmothers have a whole spectrum of reactions to their minority status. Some claim it has little or no impact on their sense of identity as women, while others believe they are profoundly affected. Those who had made early decisions or experienced minimal angst, such as Barbara Cowan, are the ones who assert most unequivocally that motherhood is irrelevant to them. "I never thought that having a child would make me a woman," said Barbara, who made an implicit joint decision with her husband when they first married. "That comes from the way I'm treated by my husband and how other people perceive me." Publicist Meredith Reynolds, who told me that she had "never put the idea of having a child into my life, never had the baby piece of the puzzle," agreed. "My choice hasn't had a bit of effect on my self-image—it simplified all of that. Being a woman and having a baby are not tied up at all for me. When people say you're not a real woman, they're taking a shot at your femininity." Marriage was more important than maternity to Robin Green, and she attributes her solid self-esteem to therapy. "I have always felt comfortable being a woman," she told me. "I've gotten good feelings from both sexes; men like me and so do women. I started therapy very young, so my sense of myself is pretty intact. I don't miss what I don't have; I'm comfortable with who I am."

Childless role models provided inspiration and validation for another vision of womanliness for many of my subjects. Tess Clark's drama coach, Eva Martinez's plantation-managing cousins, and director Paula Holbrook's "strong and childless" aunts led the way for their protégées. This was the case for Sharon Powers, a freelance magazine writer from Madison, Wisconsin. Sharon lost her mother to cancer at an early age and was raised by a stepmother who was involved with only her own children. Sharon credits her mother's childless older sister, a schoolteacher whom she "idolized," with helping her develop her individuality. "Because of her, I never thought I needed motherhood to make me whole," she said; having someone to emulate made her own feelings more acceptable.

Nonetheless, some women, including those who know they did the right thing, continue to feel incomplete or inadequate without children. Diana Russo told me that she "can pat myself on the back that I don't feel compelled or obliged," but she still projects her self-criticism onto others. "A part of me feels unfinished," she admitted. "I have the unconscious assumption that people walk around thinking you're not a woman unless you've had a baby. My therapist expected me to do it; she got pregnant during my treatment." Julie Stratton described what it feels like to be the only one of her contemporaries seriously considering a familyless life. "I fear I'm missing out on a whole experience that goes along with being a woman. It's like sitting on the sidelines of an ice hockey game. I can root on the sidelines, but I'll never be out there with the hockey stick. When so many other people are doing it, it's hard to feel normal about not doing it, but I've always been set apart." Julie's sense of alienation is still acute.

Younger women such as Julie tend to worry more about future regrets. Actress Linda Krystal, whose life has been full and successful in the years since she made her decision, now has a more philosophical attitude. "Although I definitely feel feminine and sexual—I play nurses and mothers as well as aristocratic bitches—I don't feel entirely a woman," Linda acknowledges. "And I did miss breast-feeding. That's something I'll never do, and I hear it can be exciting and satisfying. I didn't experience some part of what life can offer, something that biologically we're meant to, but at this point it's too late to turn back. I wanted to be focused on my marriage and on acting, and I'm doing both. My sense of validation comes much more from my career than it could from giving birth."

A process of revising their self-image and their view of motherhood happens for many women when they finally make up their minds. Sometimes, as was the case for me, they notice the changes only after the fact. Long after filmmaker Jackie Fast's revelatory conversations with her renovation helper and her gynecologist and the country weekend she and her husband spent with boisterous children—incidents that spanned several years— she amended her former position. "I used to assume because that's what women did, I'd be missing something if I didn't. Then it was more like a part of being female, like having a mammogram—not the most pleasant experience, but part of the deal. This co-resided in my mind with knowing that I didn't enjoy kids, never wanted to hold them or thought they were cute. I hear about women feeling empty or guilty, but I never really cared about what other people thought." By the time Jackie resolved her ambivalence, she "never looked back, never had any more conflict." Jackie's history of embracing her nonconformity, in contrast to Julie's uneasiness with hers, eased Jackie's way.

Dina Kahn also described a process of coming to terms that left her feeling liberated and comfortable with herself, her former distress yielding to a sense of accomplishment. "In my late thirties," Dina related. "I went through lots of depression. I'd make up my mind and then reconsider. I spent many years doing this until I realized I was trying to talk myself into it. When I got to the point where I finally was at the end of the whole process and I felt one hundred percent comfortable and strong, I felt wonderful; grieving was along the way."

The choice not to have a child is never neutral, the way the choice of one profession or another can be; too much is at stake. Making so unpopular a decision means stepping outside society's norms. It is an active rejection of something fundamental and expected—a reaction against motherhood as well as an embracing of childlessness. Not surprisingly, women who do it often view motherhood negatively or give more weight to aspects of maternity that seem unappealing or oppressive to them. They do this to bolster their own position, to justify and defend themselves, and because this is the truth as they see it. The natural human tendency to avoid cognitive dissonance—to explain away evidence that would undermine a conflict that has been resolved at a price—contributes to the defensiveness and mutual, if usually subtle, biases of mothers and nonmothers.

One thing childless women *don't* seem to worry about is their sex appeal. Not only do they consider themselves just as attractive and desirable as women with children; concern about the negative impact of motherhood on their love life is one of the most common reasons they give for not having families in the first place. In their eyes, motherhood is unsexy. "I feel more attractive and feminine because I don't have children," lawyer Janet Frank proclaimed. "Maternity is the antithesis of that." According to Jackie Fast, "being a mother wouldn't make me feel appealing; I get that from the mirror and from men's reactions."

Moonlighting as a belly dancer "guarantees" photographer Sandra Singer's allure. She believes that many mothers lose interest in that aspect of their womanliness. "I've seen too many women who have children lose their sexuality as well as their identity. They let their bodies go, and they complain about their husbands' sexual advances. I complain about the lack." Like many women I interviewed, Sandra thinks of pregnancy primarily as an emotionally disruptive and physically distorting state she is glad to miss. She also objects, professionally as well as personally, to the bizarre excesses of exhibitionism that can accompany giving birth and which are rarely criticized. "I find current notions of high-tech childbirth offensive," she told me. "If you don't produce a home video with the entire family present and your crotch as the star, you're not comfortable with your body."

Marty Richardson summarized the potent positive effect that making an active choice not to be a mother has had on her sense of being female. "It enhances my womanhood and sexuality because I feel more like an individual, separate from anybody else: it makes me more powerful as a woman—and I'll also be able to explore the masculine part of my personality more as a result." For Marty, femininity is psychic as much as physical. "My sexuality is not just my reproductive organs; it's my mind and my soul." Not having children, Marty contends, has freed her to become a more complete human being.

No matter how content she is with herself or how sensual she feels, every voluntarily childless woman must contend with the virtually universal perception that her behavior brands her as selfish and deficient in the capacity for unconditional love, the womanly virtue most traditionally associated with mothering. That all of my subjects mentioned it—either to refute it angrily, to defend themselves against the charge, or to assert it proudly and in some cases defiantly—indicates how deeply ingrained is the assumption that any real woman ought to possess limitless reserves of altruism, which are manifested in the desire to care for children.

Literary agent Pam Hall breezily describes herself as an "advocate of selfishness." "Women feel guilty because they think not having children is an abdication of responsibility and it's selfish. It sounds awful, but I like to please myself first. I think certain people are naturally nurturing, selfless, giving—I'm none of those things, except when I want to be, and then I am completely." Pam means that she needs to be in charge of the conditions under which she gives her all, and that as a mother this would be impossible.

Acupuncturist Anna Lincoln is also unapologetic. "People have said mine is a selfish way of life. Yes—I want to live in a way that suits my own rhythm. I don't want to be a slave to my pediatrician. If that's selfish, then self-knowledge is selfish. I think it's a stupid definition."

Sales representative Nora Adams redefines selfishness in terms that make sense for her. "It gets me mad when other people try to make me feel guilty and say I'm selfish. You should only call somebody selfish if she isn't giving to a child she has." Fund-raiser Hope Walker points out that, contrary to popular sentiment, motherhood is no guarantee of selfless behavior. "People associate being adult and responsible with having children," she says, "but I know a woman who's divorcing her third husband and has children with all three. Isn't there any other criterion?"

"I'm fiercely nurturing," insists Tess Clark, citing her experiences caring for dying friends and teaching dance to nursing home residents. Tess adamantly refutes the assumption that mothers have a monopoly on compassion. "I'm able to give unconditional love from a very real place in ways many people assume only mothers can, and I resent that they think that." Although she agrees with Tess on a rational level, innkeeper Nancy Sherman still can't help worrying that her lack of desire to take care of a baby is a poor reflection on her. "I fear it shows a lack of generosity, which is important to my self-image," Nancy admitted. This is one of the reasons that she considers it her "responsibility to serve as a role model for younger women." "I want to present myself to them, to encourage them, as a counterpoint to everybody who's having kids, to say, 'There's a different way and I'm doing it and it works.' " Her desire to offer this kind of support is a combination of compensation, self-expression, and caretaking.

Amy Brandon, the crime reporter, takes a different tack. She believes that mothers really do give consistently in ways she cannot and in return are able to have experiences that she must relinquish. "I have moments where just to be giving is a wonderful feeling," she said wistfully. "It's motivated millions of people. You lose that transcendent moment. To be a mother is to be a total caregiver, maybe the only way to experience that, so I won't have it." This loss is the price she pays for choosing a more self-oriented way of life.

What makes it acceptable for childless women such as Amy to deal with missed opportunities is their awareness of the love and intimacy they have in their own lives. As nutritionist Cindy Gardner said, "it's possible that having children helps you discover a good part of yourself that you didn't know about more than if you didn't have them, that they reveal your capacity to give love. But I know that I have it anyway."

Exercising that capacity when there is no small recipient available at home requires childless women to seek alternatives. They find all sorts of ways to nurture others, both children and adults, strangers and relatives, and they speak of these relationships as some of the most meaningful in their lives. Robin Green helped raise her neighbor's son and watches over her elderly former employer. "I haven't missed having children because I've taken care of all these people," she said. "They supplement. There's a lot of nurturing in my life." Accountant Lisa Diamond delights in the role of favorite aunt. "Having connections to young people is important, and I have it with my sister's children. I cultivate it, because it makes you grow and helps you see the world in a new way. Each generation has things to teach the older one."

Jane Michaels chose child psychiatry as her specialty because she wanted to have a direct healing influence on troubled children. "I got my M.D. so that I could make a contribution that way," she told me. "I won't have my own child, but I'll have lots of other people's and also be able to go out at night. It's just as valid."

Journalist Diana Russo wants to use her love and knowledge of literature to make contact with children. "My relationship to children can take a different form.

My pleasure and plan for the future is teaching poetry to children in my country house. I'm going to set up a little school. I won't suckle children at my breast, but I will have a relationship with them as a substitute."

Just because a woman prefers the company of adults ("Bring the kids to me when they turn eighteen," Barbara Cowan said) does not mean that she has no need to nurture. Barbara loves fostering the talent of the artists she represents, just as child psychiatrist Jane Michaels derives profound gratification from being the symbolic parent for her patients, who are "other people's children." Paula Holbrook takes great pride in the maternal aspect of her work as a director. "Working with the people I have associated with has been a creative experience. I'm good at getting the best out of people. A great actress told me recently that I had really helped her; maybe that's my way of mothering." Law student Nina Andrews anticipates satisfaction in a maternal role in the future. "Having a mentor relationship with a younger woman will fulfill me just as much as being a mother," she predicts.

The foundation of these women's self-possession and self-awareness, the factor that every one of them considered fundamental, is that they purposely and deliberately chose the lives they lead. This knowledge helps them overcome prejudice and create a fulfilling sense of their identity as women, beyond motherhood. The act of choice confers on them the feeling of being in charge of their own destinies, belief in themselves, and a sense of power.

Lisa Diamond is proud that she thought motherhood over seriously and made a conscious decision against it. "Many women produce babies without thinking about it. I strongly believe that no one should have children to fill in a gap. Now that women have a choice it's sadder when they don't exercise it because of external pressure, but you have to be stubborn to resist. I think many women are not cut out to be mothers—maybe it's just as innate not to. Now I know there's nothing wrong with it; it's just who I am."

Coming to her own conclusion, as her therapist advised her, has turned out well for Christy Nichols. "It came from a sense of who I was and what I needed," Christy realized. "Not having children has given me the ability to do everything I want, to go after my career, which I adore, to be productive."

For Anna Lincoln, "life really did begin at forty," the age at which she remarried and made her final decision. "I feel no stigma," Anna informed me. "I think that really comes from within, a reflection of ambivalence and guilt. Not being a mother has enabled me to be me, the me I always knew I was. Too many people grow up without introspection." Despite the unsolicited warning she received, Nora Adams feels "grateful" for the life her decision made possible. "I don't have children by design, and I've been able to enrich my own life and my husband's by not having them," she said. "Having done it takes a weight off; there's a certain peace. It's put away, so I don't have to worry about it. I can make my own life."

Embracing the decision can be liberating even in retrospect. Leslie Harriman, a stylish and influential fifty-year-old owner of a Manhattan art gallery, has been prominent in her field for years, but only recently has she had the courage to publicly proclaim that she is childless by choice. "I felt a stigma in my earlier years," Leslie confessed. "I was afraid that people would judge me or feel sorry for me—I didn't realize then that the stigma comes from backlash, from mistrusting a decision to be different. But now when someone asks about it, I make a point of saying, 'I've chosen not to be a mother.' I made that choice out of strength." Leslie's recognition that she had really done what she had wanted to all along was the essence of the woman she had become.

Chapter 7

What We Leave Behind:

Aging and Nonbiological Legacies

MAKING A WILL WITH NO HEIR IS A LONELY, SOBERING EXPERI-ence. Mortality becomes concrete for anybody who signs that document, but somehow my childlessness made death seem even more absolute. Already I have amassed an incredible number of possessions: Who gets them? Who will want them? I began to understand—even to envy—the poignant pleasure and comfort my mother gets from showing me her things, encouraging me to take Italian plates and Navajo rugs, the ponderous sterling flatware service for twelve my Russian grandmother earmarked for me on her deathbed, the six pairs of custom-made forties platform shoes that would probably fit, reminiscing about each piece as she offers it to me. These objects embody memories for both of us; they are my family's artifacts, the bearers of history and personality. At the end of my life these things and my additions will evoke no such allusions for their new owners.

Bequeathing money is easier and arouses much less anxiety, because my cash is no different from anybody else's. It can do some good for causes I believe in, such as educating future therapists, but it bears no stamp of individuality, no reflection of me. The accoutrements of my life are what fill and define my world, whose collective meaning will be lost forever when I am gone.

My earrings are the biggest problem. A friend (who will inherit some of them) teased me that "SHE HAD EARRINGS TO DIE FOR" should be my epitaph. This eclectic collection is the most personal, idiosyncratic thing I own—witty (bunches of lush black plastic grapes, hamburgers with sesame seed buns that a little boy on a bus asked if I had gotten at McDonald's, purple polka-dotted pocketbooks), spectacular (a New York vista including the Brooklyn Bridge, the Chrysler Building, and other landmarks; metallic gold sun faces hung with the signs of the zodiac; six-inch-long aluminum lightning bolts with balls on the end that hit me in the teeth once when I was running for a taxi), joyous (3-D enameled jungle animals, a sea turtle and two starfish, subtly sparkling black-beaded tassels, cascades of glass bubbles filled with colored liquids like old apothecary bottles). Native girls in Java had pointed approvingly to the bananas hanging from my ears, and once when I had finished my first lecture of the semester and asked the class for questions, a bold student said, "Why aren't you wearing earrings—they're legendary?"

Having no material as well as no genetic continuity is a reality that I must accept as one of the consequences of the life I have chosen. Besides, I'm not accepting everything my own mother offers me, only what suits me;

no child incorporates or perpetuates her parents in their entirety. The best I can do is take delight while I can in the beloved objects and adornments that surround me and leave them to people whose lives they will continue to embellish in my memory, though my beneficiaries do not bear my name and some of them may not live much longer than I do. I must recognize that my connections to my possessions, like my relationships with people I love, are no less meaningful because they are finite.

Lauren Mansfield pondered a similar problem when she became executrix of her mother's estate: without an obvious heir herself, what would she leave and to whom when her own time came? "The future's been on my mind since then," she told me. "Death is so final." The experience also caused her to think about the impact of her choice on her whole life, for better and for worse. Being childless had given her the opportunity to contemplate and had created the necessity to do so.

Lauren is the most outwardly traditional of any woman I spoke to, since she is the only one without a current job and is being supported by her husband. Lacking the family responsibilities that occupy most full-time housewives, the forty-nine-year-old sportswoman and self-described "contrarian" lives on a scenic bluff near Yakima, Washington, where she divides her time between white-water rafting and community organization. Until recently, her closest friends and fellow activists were older couples whose children were grown, since everybody else her age in the area was raising a family.

Lauren had had a feeling that parenthood wasn't for her since adolescence, when she selected "Zero Population Growth" as the topic for her first research paper. She acknowledges the losses and the gains her way of living entails. "I know I'm missing a lot—the growth that occurs in you when you are trying to help a child grow. There's a kind of self-knowledge you only get from having kids, a whole range of experience, which I had to some degree when I taught school; it stretches you. You see the world through another's eyes." But she knows she acquired something rare and precious as a result: "time to reflect on ways of being that most people don't have."

Lauren did a lot of reflecting while she sat at her mother's bedside during her last illness. Like so many women I talked to, she had made being different from her mother—a strict Norwegian immigrant who was trained as a physician but never practiced medicine—a lifelong goal. Only in retrospect did she realize how well she had succeeded. She had labored her whole life not to emulate her neglectful mother, who had been so afraid that her husband would be killed in World War II that she followed him to the European front, leaving Lauren with her grandparents for an entire year. When her mother later fell sick, Lauren had to take charge of a household of six.

Unlike Tammy Lyons's mother, who came to appreciate her daughter at the end of her life, Lauren's mother saw Lauren's not having children as an unforgivable slight, a repudiation; this was partially true. But self-awareness helped Lauren not take the accusation personally, because she recognized that it was a projection of her mother's disappointment in her own life. "I am different enough from her that I could actually hear that and reject it instead of internalizing it." Now, as an adult, she had the insight to observe her mother more objectively and to help her all the same. "When I was taking care of her before she died, I saw I really wasn't like her," Lauren recollected sadly but confidently.

Just as her mother's life motivated Lauren to live differently, her mother's death made her resolve to bequeath a better legacy than she had received: "There's a piece of property we own. I would like that to become a public park—there's some sort of spiritual quality about the place, and it's something we could leave in our name. The other thing I want to do is to build an addition to our local library. I believe so strongly in community."

By bestowing gifts of beauty and wisdom this child of a nongiving mother became a giving nonmother, completing the process of separation and becoming herself through what she vowed to pass down to people she would never know.

"Who will take care of me when I'm old and ill?" is the scary question every childless woman asks herself. She doesn't have a daughter like Lauren to turn to, and she knows that there is a high probability she will outlive her husband. If, like me, she has no extended family, she had better make her own arrangements in advance. "That's why I've got lots of insurance," Jackie Fast told me with a nervous laugh.

Temperament and experience determine how a childless woman regards her future. Visiting her childless aunt in a nursing home gave fashion stylist Christy Nichols a chilling glimpse of the fate that could await her too. "She's all alone in that place," Christy told me soberly, still shaken by the encounter. "After I saw her I sat on my bed and cried because I pictured myself like her, with nobody there." Despite the satisfactions of her own life and her certainty that she had been right to follow her own inclination with her therapist's encouragement, she couldn't get that image out of her mind.

Newly remarried nurse Anita Stark also frets about the

future, but her concerns are mitigated by her recently augmented array of relatives and her naturally optimistic disposition. "I think about nobody taking care of me 'cause there's nobody left," Anita acknowledged, "but I can't help believing that something will work out. My extended family will be there for me, so I don't get too worried."

Holidays are recurrent times of reckoning for a woman without a family; a Thanksgiving dinner for two (or worse, for one) doesn't fit the Norman Rockwell ideal. Former professor Susan Bartlett felt this particularly after she retired from teaching and moved to a small community in the South. "Toward the end of the year I feel the loss of having no ready-made family to celebrate with," she said. "Sometimes I worry that my friends feel they have to invite me." Beverly Goodman, a fifty-year-old television producer, has a realistic attitude toward her holiday blues. "As I've gotten older and my family has died—six people in the last five years—I suddenly see what used to be a large family with everybody gone. Nobody's there on holidays, no presents and fun, when there used to be ten or twelve people. It's very sad. Of course I have concerns about where I'll go for Christmas when I'm old, but I couldn't be a mother and live my life with the notion that I'm hating this today but I'll love it tomorrow." Actress Linda Krystal expressed a similar sentiment about life's inevitabilities. "My one dumb regret—because it's not a good reason to have a child—is what will it be like dying. I fear dying alone, but I suppose everyone does anyway, even if you have a family."

Personality has as much influence as family circumstances do on how a woman copes with the trials of aging. Says writer Joyce Rogers, "Maybe when I'm old, I'll feel more alone than I do now, but I have a tendency to feel lonely anyway, and it doesn't have to do with whether I have a child; it's my temperament." Sharon Powers sees solitude very differently: "I'm not afraid of the future, because I'll never be lonely as long as there's a book to read."

These women understand that the desire to raise a child, not anxiety about their own futures, is the only good reason to have one, and they also know that offspring are no guarantee of security at the end of life. As Barbara Cowan put it, "Being old is a crummy thing either way—I don't imagine for one moment that having children would make it better. Nobody knows really how children will treat you. You can't count on anything from them, and it might be an unpleasant discovery." Acupuncturist Anna Lincoln agrees. "I've seen enough old people in senior citizen centers who have children to be aware it doesn't matter. If you don't stay close to your biological family out of love and devotion, no guilt trip will make it work." Pam Hall noted in her brash, ironic way, "I find it very rare that comfort from family in old age comes true. I think it's a slight delusion, one of those American myths; maybe it used to hold when we all lived in little towns. Mostly parents become burdens to their children. I won't miss having children to aggravate, nobody to think, 'Oh, God, who gets her now?' And because I have my own strong extended family, I will never want for relations. If I wanted to have a huge Thanksgiving, I have lots of relatives to invite—not that I've ever done it."

Their husband is the only family member many of these women have, and this relationship is so close that the prospect of losing it looms especially large. Robin Green, who married a much older mate later in life, knows what's in store. "It's not getting older without children that bothers me," she said. "It's losing Jack. I'm going to be a young widow." Director Paula Holbrook has already been one—and it was her friends who got her through. "My friends became my family," Paula told me, recalling the terrible period when she underwent surgery and lost her husband and mentor shortly afterward. "During the whole thing my friends were incredible. They're the ones I can call on and count on. They're my contemporaries—that's the new reality." After her accident, horticulturist Eva Martinez also turned to her friends. "When I was going through rehabilitation, I didn't go to my parents. Because of that I don't feel I'm going to be alone later either," she told me confidently.

Friends replace family as the lifelines for the majority of the women I met. They fill in for children, siblings, and even parents, providing comfort and support through all the crises of life that others look to relatives for or wish they could. My own experience during my husband's life-threatening illness taught me that no blood relations could be more giving or devoted than my dear friends.

One of the ways publicist Meredith Reynolds has vowed to be different from her mother is in the way she conducts her friendships. "I have deep relationships lasting more than twenty-five years," she says. "My friendships are the most important thing in my life—I watched my mother cut herself off from friends. She'd turn away from people if they hurt her; I don't want to live that way." Marty Richardson sees having relationships based on interest and affection rather than accidental biological connection as a cornerstone of her life and her hope for the future. "Because I felt I was stuck with my family, I want to choose the people I want to be around later on. Why be held hostage—why not continue to make friends and have relationships, not blood ties, all your life?"

There is a viable alternative to the traditional ideal of the matriarch surrounded by her children: the older woman with a warm and caring circle of peers of all ages. Barbara Cowan has achieved this. "It would be grand to grow old with friends," she says at sixty-six. "I have a lot of young ones, and I expect them to be around, just as loyal, so I'll have my friends for the next twenty to thirty years."

Not having a family doesn't necessarily lead to a loveless demise like Christy's great aunt's—not if you plan like choreographer Tess Clark has. Instead of identifying with the image of a sick elderly woman abandoned by the world, Tess has made it her business to guarantee— as far as is humanly possible—a very different scenario for herself:

"I was in a hospital recently and saw an old woman being admitted wheeled in on a gurney. 'Who can we notify?' they asked her. 'Do you have a next of kin or a child?'—and I saw myself. God willing, if it's me on that gurney, I'll be able to recite twenty phone numbers. What made me sad for her is that she didn't have a soul; they would fly to me. It made me appreciate the network I've spent thirty years reinforcing. The safety net is critical."

By carefully building a nucleus of loving connections based on choice and commitment, Tess assures herself that she will have as much sustenance and security as any mother could hope for.

Childlessness not only means having no progeny to take care of you or carry on your name; nobody will carry on your dreams either. What you do has to be accomplished by you and you alone. Women without children must face earlier and more directly than others the limits of their possibilities, the things left eternally

173

undone. They have no one to project hopes onto or to correct mistakes or to achieve what they could not or dared not. They cannot comfort themselves with the fantasy that their children's future successes will repair their own past defeats.

The demands of a radically self-reliant childless life scare thirty-two-year-old aspiring playwright Simonetta Fracci. "What if I wake up at fifty and say, 'You blew it?' " she asked. *"What if I fail at my writing?"* Many women still believe that they have a fallback position, the option of making parenthood the basic source of meaning in their lives. As some of the stories I heard testify, when a mother's frustration and sense of failure go underground, both she and her children feel the consequences.

Having aspirations for the next generation is part of being a good parent, and raising a reasonably sane child is something to be proud of. But a child has a separate identity and is a very different sort of "achievement" from a work of art. Simonetta has to face the fact that if she gives up writing and decides to have a child instead and her child writes a Pulitzer Prize–winning play, it doesn't mean Simonetta did. Motherhood will not protect her from that reality, and she'll still be responsible for what she makes of her own life.

Retired drama coach Karen Gold understands how important a sense of autonomy is for a woman, particularly as she gets older. She made her own choice at age twenty, in 1946, when she decided to marry and go on the road with a poor but charming vaudeville performer, a situation far too unstable for a family. After years on tour, she and her husband settled down and Karen brought in most of the money teaching theater and directing plays in a Buffalo, New York, high school. When her husband died, she retired to rural Vermont, where she writes, rides her horses, and had a long love affair in her sixties with a man in his forties. "Whether or not you have a child, the problem every woman has to face is always her own identity and self-esteem," said Karen. "Some mothers give up struggling and try to find fulfillment only in their children. That's an abdication. If you use motherhood as a distraction, it never works." Now she comes into Bennington weekly to attend a workshop on Shakespeare, comfortably socializing with actors of all ages. "I have to work to maintain my independence and conviction," she told me. "I have the possibility of a good end of my life if I don't lose my nerve." The legacy she wants to leave is her "clear mind."

To choose a childless life is to face personal limitations on many levels—to realize that your needs differ from the majority of other people's, that your priorities are at odds with what much of the world expects of you, that your freedom is priceless but has its costs. To acknowledge that you are unwilling or unable to undertake everything a woman is now supposed to is sober, realistic, and an enormous relief. Women who fully accept this recognize that they have not experienced everything in life and see that nobody else does either—or needs to. Songwriter Marty Richardson believes "it's a lie to think you can have it all. Young women of the nineties expect to do it all, and if they can't, they feel like less—it's horrible to have that guilt." In contrast to the image of the driven superwoman, fund-raiser Hope Walker asserts, "My life is full; I don't have everything, but I feel no need to redo what I didn't do."

Contrary to Simonetta's fears, nobody I spoke to who was past her childbearing years feels she "blew it" by not having a baby; they've all come to terms. Once they made up their minds and dealt with their losses, they went on with their lives, strengthened and energized by the process. And they're full of plans for their later years: Diana Russo will start her private poetry school, Pam Hall intends to study literature and become more active in feminist politics, and casting director Myra Wyeth plans to get in front of the footlights once again. "Since everybody in my family lives into their nineties, I'll be around long enough to do it," she predicts. The act of choosing was liberating for every one of them, even for the few who claimed that they would consider motherhood now if they were ten years younger. "Working this through was one of the only good things about turning forty," Cindy Gardner remarked.

Most voluntarily childless women feel reconciled and self-accepting, proud and confident. Many think they have forfeited something, but all know they have gained independence, intimacy, and focus. Quite a few have done things that family life would have made difficult or foolhardy. As war correspondent Rachel Randolph put it, "Would I have gone into Afghanistan with the guerillas if I had a child waiting at home?" Over time, the compensations loom much larger than the losses. There is a certain note of relaxation and appreciation when they look back at the impact of their decision. "If I ever had a scintilla of concern, it's gone now," Pam Hall said. "If parenting had become the focus of my life, it would have sidetracked a lot of other creativity." Barbara Cowan saw how right her decision would still be and what it has made possible for her. "At times I look back and wonder what I would have done if there had been good child care. I'm sure the answer is still no. I wanted to live in the company of adults. Most of the things I've done in my life I wouldn't have been able to do with children."

"The generational thing" still bothers Simonetta. "Not passing down something is very sad; I cherish the relationship I have with my mother. If you haven't had a family, you've lost something you would have had, but there are other ways to pass things on." Grief and promise are intermingled for many of them. Nora Adams is also sorry that "my life experience will stop with one person," but she's glad to be "an explorer with a passion for new experiences." Stockbroker Mimi Davis's regrets are "few and isolated." "When I see the right little kid in a stroller, it's kind of painful," she admits. "Although I don't know how I'd fit it in. I'm wistful, but it lasts five minutes." Retired psychology professor Susan Bartlett believes that "being spared the responsibility of having to put others first and sacrifice my needs and preferences for a small human being reinforced my natural tendency to be introspective." Acknowledging the losses makes these women mindful of their accomplishments.

Women come to terms with the choices they've made in their own unique ways. Textile designer Michiko Nicholson, who was born in Japan and moved to the United States as a teenager, has an unusual point of view. "I never see myself as childless," asserts this tiny, vivid woman who decided in her early thirties by marrying a man who'd had a vasectomy. "This is because I have such strong feelings about the deep personal connections between and among people, which go beyond origins, circumstances, or the usual structure of things. I make the rounds of babies and dogs in my building every day—it's great fun." As for regrets, she says philosophically, "I can't say I don't have any regrets—no one can, and I do wonder about the different kind of life I would have had, an alternative choice I could have made. I can only smile at the personality of the unknown, possibly wonderful thing I never saw, and I have no remorse, absolutely none." And Rachel, because she *did* go into Afghanistan and many other places, relishes the adventures she's had. "I feel sure I would have been a good mother, but all the things that have gone on in my life would not have gone on; my opportunities wouldn't have been open. I can't say I've had regrets, because I've loved my life. I've had such an eventful time, I wouldn't mind dying now."

Parents don't have to worry whether they will leave a legacy; part of them automatically lives on in their children. The childless are denied that sense of posterity. Their heritage—whether it's something as concrete as a park or a painting or as intangible as a relationship or an act of compassion—cannot be biologically based.

Some women cited concrete achievements—the books they had written, the plays they had directed or starred in, the films they made. For others, what really counted was the relationships they had forged. Many wanted to be remembered for their experiences, their accomplishments, their conviction that they were going to leave the world better than they had found it. They feel that they gave of themselves and got a great deal back. Getting through to others, expressing themselves, making a difference on a personal scale—these are the things they leave. Overall, their joy in living every day mattered most.

Creative endeavors were central to the lives of many of the women I met, and the process itself was as important as the final product. Only in the exclusivity of their focus do they differ from mothers who are artists. Tammy Lyons, who now has her mother's blessing and the marriage she always wanted, will leave her paintings. But the actual canvases matter less to her than the passionate self-expression that produces them. "It's not important that my work be for the ages," Tammy told me. "I'm glad I made my paintings, because I think that life is for living day to day. They mean something to me and make me proud, because for me art is the best way to express love, hate—everything. I love life so much!"

On the other hand, Tess Clark is hungry for fame. She's glad that her legacy won't be biological, but will be a vision of what's special about her personality and her talent. "I wouldn't want a clone of my life and my mistakes," she said frankly. "What I want to leave behind is my dances. I'd like to be remembered as a flamboyant artist. I have a fantasy of someday being listed in *Who's Who in American Women.* When I first saw that book, I felt a shudder because it gave credibility to a woman's life—even though there are probably a lot of assholes and wasted lives in there, they're the minority. I want to be an important woman in history." Tess also wants to have an impact on a personal level. "I'll leave a number of people who will remember that I was their first and best teacher."

Jackie Fast loves the idea that she'll be able to move people with her films, even after she's gone. "I'm leaving much more of a legacy than any child could be—I leave my work. When I make films and people see them and they change people's minds—what a rush!" And Marty Richardson is transforming her essence into music. "I'm a lyricist, so my songs will last forever. Creating them is my little kids," she said with pride.

Relationships count the most, because this is the arena where everyone has a powerful impact. "I'm going to leave a lot of love to a lot of people," said Robin Green. "I am there for a lot of people. My friends and extended family are the only thing that's really important." Meredith Reynolds, whose long-lasting friendships are the joy of her life, believes that "how I'm remembered by the people whose lives I've touched is the only legacy I've ever wanted."

Pam Hall, frank, funny, and a consummate realist, has this to say about the future: "I have an irreverent attitude toward what I will leave behind; I think we're all just infinitesimal specks of dust. Unless your child is Albert Einstein, if there are one hundred people that stand out from the hundreds of millions who have come and gone that's a lot. In one hundred years the earth will be populated by all new people, so what difference does it make?

"The meaning of my life is that I want to affect the people whose lives I touch in a very small and intimate group. I don't want to change the world or leave behind a great accomplishment. In my tiny little way I want to turn people around a bit. I never want to feel I didn't say I love you, and I want to do it when it means something. I think it has a rippling effect. This is the best anybody can do." What counts for Dina Kahn is "the difference I've made in other people's lives. The only difference between a mother and me is I'm not saying, 'I own this one.'"

A woman does not have to be a mother to give life to others. Susan Bartlett literally made the difference between life and death for her students when she counseled them. "I enabled ten or twelve young women to pass through a severe crisis in their lives. I prevented a couple of suicides. It's a source of pride that they keep in touch with me," she said with quiet dignity. Her former students, one of whom is advertising executive Julie Stratton, feel inspired by her.

Service gives meaning to the lives of women as young as Nina Andrews and as mature as Mimi Davis and Christy Nichols. Their childless status often focuses the direction these efforts take. Christy serves on the board of a YWCA shelter for battered women, where she feels she "helps women to make their own choices, to make their lives easier and better." She also is planning to finance the education of the teenage daughter of a needy friend. As a prospective feminist lawyer, Nina believes "I need a future, but it doesn't mean I have to be up to my elbows in Play-Doh. I hope I can change this screwed up world a little bit through my legal work, help people in my little community, and improve some women's lives."

Mimi Davis views not having obligatory biological heirs as an opportunity rather than a handicap; she'll be able to choose freely what to do with her money. "We don't even have a dog to leave it to. It's nice when you can do what you want with it, as opposed to knowing you have to leave it to a child. I know I'll find somebody that's needy; it wouldn't be so bad to leave everything for AIDS research. Meanwhile, I'll have a good time and a good life."

Anna Lincoln's existential attitude, her sense that life in the present is what really matters, is shared by many of my interviewees: "It's enough that I have lived. I achieved this life, I got it. It's going the way I want it to go. I always said I want to be a grown-up, and I've achieved that, which is more than most do. I've always been a problem solver for a lot of people, and that will be remembered. I've alleviated some suffering, taken some pain away through acupuncture. And in my family I'm the one who thinks deeply and comes up with solutions. I'm the glue—this is a tremendous achievement."

The finest legacy we childless women leave is our lives themselves—the love we have given and received, the fulfilled commitments to ourselves and to others. We have faced what we really feel and tried to create responsible lives that are also genuinely responsive to our own needs; we know who we are. Awareness and involvement in the world are the precious gifts we give our spiritual heirs.

We are the first generation of women who have intentionally gone beyond motherhood by our own will. We pass on to future generations a new image of femininity, a transformed notion of what it means to be a fulfilled woman, and the promise of expanded horizons. Echoing the sentiment of Rachel Randolph, we can say with confidence born of experience, pride based on self-examination, and self-knowledge derived from embracing the limits as well as the possibilities caused by our choice: "My life is my child."

Epilogue →

If You're Considering Childlessness

THE WOMEN WHOSE STORIES YOU HAVE READ IN THIS BOOK offer the best advice you can get on how to go about deciding whether or not to have a baby: personal experience. Cultivating an inquiring and honest emotional attitude can help you apply these insights to your own life.

Would motherhood suit you? Don't postpone asking yourself this question, even if it's hard to answer. Really think about it, starting now. Make time to do this. In order to choose wisely, it's important to know as much as possible about your feelings, your conflicts, your fantasies, and your needs. Talk to your husband, talk to your friends, and most important, talk to yourself—and listen carefully, with an open mind, to what you say.

1. How do you really feel about children? Women who are not suited for motherhood can have a whole gamut of reactions, ranging from acute dislike to pleasure and delight. Does it make you uncomfortable or annoyed to be around kids more often than not? If so, is your reaction based mostly on inexperience and awkwardness—which can change—or are there deeper causes for your discomfort? And even if you love the company of children, do you really enjoy their interests and activities for extended periods? Are you prepared to spend much of your time participating in them or arranging them?

Tell yourself the truth. If your feelings are mixed, try to live with your ambivalence without denying either pole; see where this takes you, which feeling is stronger. If you discover that the negative predominates, don't assume you'll get used to it. That depends on the intensity of your aversive reaction and how motivated you are to change. Ask yourself why you feel as you do, of course, but don't expect the downside to simply go away.

2. Never assume that any problem in your life will be solved by having a baby—except a longing for a baby. Are you trying to cement a marriage, buy old-age insurance, fit in because everybody else is doing it, or avoid disappointment? Are you looking to a child to give meaning to your life? Becoming a mother for any of these reasons is guaranteed to backfire on everybody concerned.

Among the problems a baby won't solve are:

An unhappy marriage
Poor self-esteem
Depression
Frustration
A sense of failure
Disappointments with job, friends, or family

For such things, only work on yourself—through thinking, talking to others, or psychotherapy and actively changing your own life—will make a difference. No one can fix your problems but you.

3. Don't let anybody talk you into pregnancy if your heart is really not in it; being a mother is an immense commitment. Do not assume that your husband will take on half the responsibility if you have a child or that having a baby-sitter will give you much more time to yourself, and make your determination accordingly.

If you find that you're leaning toward motherhood, expect your life to change profoundly. Living with a baby entails giving up certain things and tolerating others. Think about what matters most to you and what you can least do without. Ask yourself these questions:

What's my sensitivity-to-intrusion quotient? How much do I need quiet and privacy?

How important to me is spontaneity and the freedom to get up and go?

How essential to me is uninterrupted intimacy with a man?

How ambitious am I professionally?

Would you deeply resent or feel bitter about giving up these things or curtailing them? Gauging your own reactions will tell you how willing you would be to make sacrifices for your child.

4. Think about your own childhood. What was good that you would want to repeat and what was bad that you want to repair? Would you make a good mother? What parental qualities do you (and your spouse) have, which do you lack, and how important are they? How much of your past do you feel you would have to over-

come in order to be a good parent and are you ready to confront it? The time to examine this is *before* you get pregnant.

5. Do any of these excuses sound familiar?

> "We can't afford a baby now."
> "My career is just taking off."
> "I'm not ready to be tied down."

If every time you think about it you find a compelling reason not to try to get pregnant, maybe you're telling yourself something. Maybe you want to keep your life as it is. Recognize and label your resistance to looking at this possibility. Feel your fear, and face it anyway.

6. Expect all kinds of intense feelings to come up when you really start thinking in earnest about intentionally never being a mother. Anxiety, depression, anger, and every unresolved issue from your childhood—including some totally unanticipated ones—can be aroused. This is normal and ultimately helpful. Allow yourself to have all your reactions now, so you won't be hit with regrets about having denied and avoided them twenty years from now. Give yourself the opportunity to work them through by expressing and attending to them. And cry if you need to; tears are part of mourning, and mourning is part of coming to terms. You are losing one of life's possibilities when you decide not to have children, even as you gain others.

It's especially important to encourage the man in your life to deal with his feelings about giving up parenthood, even if he has difficulty doing so, and even if it's hard for you to hear about it when he does. Something this central to a relationship requires a joint resolution.

7. If on reflection you do conclude that a family is not for you, accept that your life will be very different from most other people's. It's not pathological to be different, even though it's harder. Choosing to forgo motherhood doesn't mean that you couldn't do it, but that you prefer another kind of life; it's not an indication that something is wrong with your capacity to love and nurture. If having a family is really not what you want, recognizing this is the mature thing to do; taking charge of your destiny is something to be proud of.

Be prepared to feel left out of the mainstream and take steps to find a peer group. Build a network, reach out; you are part of a growing group of women who made the same decision. They can validate your choice in the present and support you in the future.

8. Having a child of your own is not the only way to ensure that close relationships with children will be part of your life. If you feel the need, there are lots of opportunities: friends and relatives who would welcome another adult in their children's world, volunteer work, and teaching.

9. Consider telling people the truth when they ask you why you don't have children. Honesty is self-affirming.

10. Don't blame yourself if you decide that motherhood is not for you—and learn not to blame your mother or other members of your family either, because if you do, you will be enchained to the past, which will siphon off energy from living in the present. Self-awareness and compassion are your best resources.

Don't expect a perfect resolution. You may still feel sad and regretful at times; so do most mothers who are candid with themselves. You won't ever regret the self-knowledge gained from facing your feelings.

Making a genuine, conscious choice is very important. No carefully considered decision, responsive to your real feelings, born of honest self-examination, will be the wrong one.

Author's Note

I would welcome comments from readers about their own experiences in choosing childlessness. Write to me at:

ICM
Attention: L. Bankoff
40 West Fifty-seventh Street
New York, NY 10019